WHERE THERE'S SMOKE

WHERE THERE'S SMOKE

A SHELLS HARBOUR MYSTERY

E.L. BOWERS

The Pickle Jar Press

Published by the Pickle Jar Press

Cover photograph by E.L. Bowers

ISBN: 978-1-9992324-1-2

First Printing, 2023

One

A grey cloud of smoke as dark as the Atlantic Ocean in winter rose above a stand of evergreens as Penny rounded a bend on her morning run. She looked up at the roiling column. On her next step, she stumbled over a loose rock that freckled the pathway.

She tumbled forward, knees grinding into the gravel, hands scraping into the dirt, breath pushed quickly from her lungs. As she fell, a figure darted out from the tree line ahead of her. Dressed in dark colours with a hood pulled over their head, Penny couldn't tell who it was.

"Hey," she called out in confusion. But the runner didn't break stride and quickly disappeared around a corner. From the woods to her left, sounds of pops punctuated the air like holiday fireworks. Penny pulled herself to her feet and picked gravel from her bare palms.

It was a rare warm winter day for Shells Harbour. The chill had lifted enough to give a glimpse of the spring that would soon come. Morning sun brought a melt that sprinkled snow drops from evergreens in light showers onto the thin jacket covering Penny's shoulders. The season of change was coming. The trail she ran on was the meandering former railway route separated from the sparse handful of houses by a line of trees and bushes thick enough to offer privacy. But old engines chugging to the lumber mill and fish plant would have been close enough to rattle teacups on kitchen tables.

Penny heard more pops, louder and more explosive. She directed her aching legs and scraped knees into the woods through a narrow path, the same route used by the person in the hooded sweater who'd startled her.

A dense, acrid smell hit. Not wood smoke, like the smell from the cast-iron stove tended by her aunt Sheila on frosty nights. Penny smelled the chemical tang of burning industrials. It could be plastic, an illegal burn of household junk or tires. That plume of smoke was bigger than a bonfire, she thought as she pushed back boughs.

It was because of her grandfather, who spent 20 years as fire chief in Shells Harbour, that Penny couldn't ignore smoke. Where there's smoke, there's fire, he would tell her, his warning that was not just about safety, but about people. About listening to signals and signs and taking them as indicators of trouble to come. It was not a worn-out cliche to her grandfather, but a life motto.

Twigs and leaves crackled under Penny's running shoes. Until a few days earlier, the woods had been buried under a foot of snow. Now they were mostly melted, save for a few patches in the darkest corners, beyond the touch of sunlight. The smell grew stronger. Penny reached into the back pocket of her running pants and pulled out her cellphone.

The trees were still thin before the budding growth of spring. Penny could see through them enough to make out the shape of a collection of buildings. She discerned what she was looking at as she got closer. Sheds, several of them. There was one with clear plastic sides that looked to be crammed full with rows of plant trays. There was another made of wide slats of wood hammered lazily together, nails stuck through the boards and one end sinking into the soft spring earth. Around the sheds was a scattered collection of pieces of metal, piled in rusting, sharp edges. There was random junk. The bench seat from an old school bus. A rusted-out refrigerator on its side.

But the yard was a distraction from the growing smoke collecting over the area. Penny rushed to the front of the property and felt her stomach twist into a knot. She saw a mobile home, about the length of a bus, with its left side engulfed in angry orange flames. It was spreading, the fire licking vinyl siding that was melting like ice cream.

She clutched her phone in her hand and began tapping the screen.

She did not know whose yard she was in and saw no signs of people or fire trucks.

"9-1-1, what's your emergency?"

"I'm in Shells Harbour, off Hatchery Road, there's a - it looks like a mobile home. It's on fire. Flames are coming from the windows," Penny said.

"Can you tell me exactly where you are?" The female voice on the other end of the phone was a practiced calm.

"I don't know. I was just running on the trail behind the houses here and I saw someone running and I saw the smoke."

Penny rushed to the front of the home and saw black numbers hammered loosely on the vinyl siding near the front door, which was still away from the flames.

"Okay, I see a number. It's 1272. 1272 Hatchery Road."

"Good, I've got the fire department on the way. Are you in danger right now? Is anyone inside the home?"

"I don't even know who lives in this house. I used to live in Shells Harbour but I was away for so long, I really don't think I know anybody here anymore," Penny said. She exhaled quickly and pinched her lips shut, chiding herself for talking too much.

"It's okay, just stay calm and stay away from the flames," the operator said. "Maybe you can go to the road and wait for the fire department. They'll be on the way soon."

The operator took Penny's name and phone number and she jogged down the dirt driveway to meet the fire trucks.

Hatchery Road was still. She strained to hear sirens clawing through the quiet as smoke billowed up from the mobile home, now hidden from her sight by a thick grove of trees that would have given the homeowner privacy. A current of thoughts swirled. Homes had owners, but no one had yet appeared to claim the trailer. Penny wondered if that was the figure she saw on the trail, emerging from the pathway.

The winter air that offered a hint of spring and had been fresh on her run. Now, it was heavy. She could only wait. Sirens finally pierced the silence and Penny bounced on the balls of her purple running shoes to see the trucks. Her palms were sore from the stumble, but she waved them over her head to signal to the first engine that arrived, its red and white lights strobing. But she needn't have. The smoke was giving off its own signals, turning darker grey like clouds bringing rolling thunder.

Penny followed the trucks up the driveway, catching the diesel engine's exhaust. At the top, firefighters were hefting cylinders attached to back straps over their gear, pulling masks over their faces as if they were heading into chemical warfare.

A man with a white helmet gestured to the masked firefighters and two of them dragged a hose to the front of the mobile home, which was now spilling flames from a broken picture window. One of them twirled his fingers in the air and Penny saw the flat hose grow round and jump into a snake that curled between the truck and the firefighters. She watched as they directed a stream of water into the window.

"Were you the 9-1-1 caller, ma'am?" Penny looked away from the house to acknowledge the senior firefighter who walked toward her after giving his commands. His face was familiar, marked with wrinkles that laid around his brown eyes and a greying moustache on his top lip. Penny couldn't be sure if he was someone she once knew, or if he was familiar in a way that everything was, since she left Toronto and came home to Shells Harbour.

"I'm Deputy Chief Paul Haines. I need you to tell me if there's any reason to think there might be people inside."

"I really don't know," Penny replied, recounting for the deputy chief how she came upon the fire, and the figure who appeared on the trail, unconcerned when she called out. He nodded and grabbed the radio mic attached to the front of his bulky beige protective coat.

"Captain Bell, get your crew ready for a primary search. I don't see Coleman's truck in the driveway, but we can't be sure he's not in there."

Captain Bell. Penny looked across the dirt driveway. A team of two firefighters, in the same gear Paul Haines wore, but with the addition of a cylinder strapped to their backs and a full face mask under their helmets, marched toward the front door of the mobile home. But instead of watching the team ready to do their work, Penny looked at the man who was leading the group of firefighters. The man who would task them with searching for a victim who may not be inside.

The first team with the hose streaming water into the mobile home made progress in turning the black roiling smoke white. But it was clear the flames still threatened to consume the building. The crew would walk into a dangerous situation, and Penny knew, very well, the man who was sending them there.

Unlike with Paul Haines, there was no doubt about this man's familiarity. Especially not when Captain Jacob Bell looked right back at her.

Two

A firefighter wearing thick black gloves reached out to jiggle the handle of the front door to the mobile home. It was locked. He took a silver bar and wedged one end in between the door and the jamb. Another firefighter swung rhythmic hits to the silver bar with the blunt end of an axe. The doorframe splintered and gave way after just a few strikes.

Deputy Chief Paul Haines had left Penny and was circling the back side of the mobile home toward the woods she had passed through. Penny had finished giving her information to him. She thought she had nothing else to offer. But she couldn't bring herself to leave just yet.

Penny had made little noise in her return to Shells Harbour. She hadn't spoken to people beyond a quick hello to the teenager making lattes in the Jungle Cafe or the customers who came into her aunt's bookstore, Brittle Pages, where Penny helped.

And she hadn't announced her return to Jacob Bell. He was one of her closest friends in high school until senior year, when Jacob got a girlfriend and Penny sharpened her focus on leaving Shells Harbour. They had been friends since the earliest grades, bonding over a love of going as high as possible on the swing set. That search for adventure took Jacob into firefighting, and took Penny far from town. But her adventure was over. She felt shame. About how she left and now, how she returned, after a decade in Toronto ended in a broken relationship and a dead career.

I knew I'd see Jacob at some point, Penny thought. But good lord, not like this. Not in my spandex and sneakers. Not when I haven't thought about what to say to him.

Paul Haines emerged again from the front of the mobile home and spoke briefly to Jacob. A gust of wind carried a lick of smoke toward Penny and she inhaled at exactly the wrong moment, breathing in the chemical air and giving herself a fit of coughs as her lungs tried to clear out the toxins.

"Are you alright?" Paul reappeared in front of Penny. Her flushed cheeks turned crimson with the coughing but she quickly nodded. "You should move further back. In fact, I'll take your information, just in case we need any more details down the road, and you can carry on with your run. You must live close by if you're on foot."

Penny wrote her name and phone number on the notepad the deputy chief handed her. "I live with my aunt on the east harbour. She owns Brittle Pages, the bookstore on Barque Lane."

"Sheila Sutherland's your aunt? My goodness," the deputy chief shook his head. "We've been over to her store a few times over the years. Alarm calls, nothing serious, although if I do recall, there was something about a toaster oven once. People said her books came out smelling like smoke for quite some time."

Penny smiled and nodded. She was still living in Toronto when Sheila got distracted by a customer and left her sandwich in the toaster oven that was too old to have a reliable shut-off. Sheila told Penny she felt foolish for the commotion on the lane that was busy with tourists visiting the shops along the downtown hub.

"I went to high school with your aunt," Paul said. "So that means you must be Penelope. Harold Pintz's granddaughter."

"It's just Penny. You knew my grandfather?"

"Of course I did. He was my first fire chief. Boy, he was rigid. Tough old man. Knew right from wrong without a doubt, though. Best fire-fighter I knew. A bunch of us here came up with Chief Pintz."

"My grandmother Ivy said she became a widow to the fire service when grandpa became chief."

"She wouldn't be the first one to think that way. Though I remember Mrs. Pintz being just as tough as the chief. She started the ladies' auxiliary. Ran that group of women as tight as her husband ran the department."

Penny smiled and looked off into the woods for a glancing moment. Both of her grandparents had been dead for almost a decade but the memory of them was distinct, as strong as the smoke that had settled into the air.

Penny handed Paul's notebook back to him and he tucked it into the front pocket of his jacket. "And your folks, are they still out west?"

The portable radio he had in his other pocket crackled to life before Penny could answer.

"DC Haines, this is Shells Harbour interior team," a muffled voice called. Penny realized it must have been a firefighter inside the home. And whoever was calling probably had on one of the fierce-looking masks that was swallowing his words. Paul took a few steps away from Penny, as if he was about to take a personal phone call in a crowded room. She couldn't discern any words of the crackled radio conversation.

Penny knew she could leave. But she was compelled to stay in place. She watched the firefighters in their movements, toward the house and back, carrying tools, repositioning the hose lines. She thought about her grandfather, who would have directed operations like this one before coming home to wrap his arms around her, holding her in his distinct smell of fire and smoke.

At that moment, Jacob fixed his blue eyes on her and cocked his head to the left, offering a slight smile. She felt like crossing the yards between them and almost began moving toward him.

"Emergency, emergency, we need help in here," barked the voice on the radio held by the deputy chief a few feet away. There was no doubt about those words. Haines sprung forward and gestured to Jacob, who had already broken eye contact with Penny and was pulling a mask over his face.

"Get a team in there. Now!"

Jacob and another firefighter readied themselves with speed and hurried into the house. Penny's stomach roiled. She clutched at her arms for warmth as the sunny sky turned overcast. The white winter was chill back in place. Snow was in the forecast and the clouds promised a storm.

Through the blackened doorway, two firefighters emerged and two more were behind them. Penny had spent years in high school staring at Jacob Bell, laughing at his jokes and drinking coffees in their spare classes. But in their gear, she couldn't tell who he was.

And then, between the two teams of firefighters, Penny realized they weren't carrying a piece of equipment or a hose. They had used their hands and arms to form a sling and were carrying a person out of the mobile home. The victim was a woman, her blond hair hung down from the head and drooping toward the ground. Haines directed them to lay the woman down on a blue tarp on the outside of the house, next to a stack of gear that was quickly pushed aside.

Penny bounced on the balls of her feet to stay warm and squeezed her arms tighter against her. That woman was in the house when she spotted the smoke. When she called 9-1-1 and the operator asked her if anyone was inside. While she was chatting with Deputy Chief Haines and looking at Jacob Bell.

When she called out to the figure who darted out from the trail.

The firefighters were performing chest compressions on the woman. Soon, Penny heard the pierce of another siren. An ambulance. Jacob had taken off his protective mask and was hovering over the woman. He tapped the shoulder of the man who was performing compressions and the firefighter quickly moved away, while Jacob slid in and began rhythmically thrusting his clenched hands against the woman's body. There was no more catching eyesight, no more smiles. The morning had turned quiet and cold. There was now only the silence of a man trying to save a woman's life.

Three

After the ambulance left the fire scene, Penny began a slow jog back to Sheila's house. She used to run as an escape in Toronto and she was getting back into the habit in Shells Harbour, after a long winter of quiet nights by the fire.

But the image of the woman being pulled out of the home persisted, hovering over every step. Penny left without speaking to Jacob. She had no words to offer him and felt, as she had since returning to Shells Harbour, that she needed to disappear. She slipped back on the trail and reversed her route. Rays of sunlight that filtered through the evergreens and splayed out on the gravel trail on the first part of her run were gone. A canopy of high, white winter clouds and a breeze that sliced through Penny's running jacket replaced any warmth there had been in the morning air.

Penny emerged from the trail and turned right on to the sidewalk at a tight four-way stop, glancing briefly around the empty intersection before darting across. She looked at the row of houses to her left as she ran, saltbox and Victorian style homes painted in shades of blue and yellow. Their steep pitched roofs would send a tumble of snow onto the sidewalk after the storm that hovered over the town.

Shells Harbour never quite felt like home for Penny. Her family had deep roots, but as a teenager the small town chafed. When she left for university in Toronto, she left it all behind, including her high school friends like Jacob Bell. And her best friend, Arlene Lowery. She had gotten married and had a child and Penny still hadn't so much as met her for a cup of coffee at the Jungle Cafe.

And, Penny thought, it wasn't as if she had a fantastic life in Toronto that she left behind. In fact, the city had done Penny in. She left willingly, and when she needed somewhere to go, Shells Harbour was the only place she thought of. Although she still wasn't sure exactly why her instinct pulled her to the hometown she once eagerly left.

Penny turned the door handle to her aunt's house. Sheila had taken her in a few months earlier when she sent a hasty message that she'd be coming back from Toronto. Penny didn't say it would be a permanent move, but she knew Sheila figured it out when she came with her little car packed with suitcases and boxes, her life in the city stuffed into the back seat of a Volkswagen.

"There you are," Sheila said. She was positioned toward the mirror that hung on a wall of the narrow kitchen, wrapping a colourful scarf around her head. Penny kicked off her cold sneakers and went to the kitchen sink to run a glass of water. Sheila finished tying her knot and turned around to face her niece. "What do you think?"

Penny gulped a mouthful of water and looked at her aunt. The scarf, in swirling shades of pink and purple, was crooked on Sheila's head. Penny wrinkled her eyebrows and tried to think of a quip to make.

Nothing came. She slunk into a padded wooden chair at the table where they normally ate breakfast together when Penny returned from her morning run, and before Sheila headed out to Brittle Pages.

"Nothing to say?" Sheila laughed until she looked more closely at Penny, who had broken eye contact and was looking down into a ripple of water in her glass. "What's wrong?"

Penny's mind flooded with the smell of the smoke, the popping roar of the blaze. And of Jacob, working furiously to save a life. She recounted the events to Sheila, who listened quietly from the other side of the table.

"And then they took her away, but it didn't seem like the ambulance was rushing," Penny said, taking a last sip of her water. Her hands shook. "I just left. I was going to talk to Jacob, but I didn't know what to say."

"I never did either," Sheila said. "Your grandfather sometimes would come home from a call and go right down into the basement. He'd be working away at his wood carvings and we knew not to disturb him till he was ready. And even then, he never talked about it. At least not with us."

Penny shook her head. "I feel awful that I didn't get there faster. I didn't call 9-1-1 faster. And I don't know who that person was running out of the bushes. They didn't look back, not even for a second."

"And you told Paul that?"

Penny nodded.

"There will probably be an investigation," Sheila said. "Maybe you should write what you remember, while it's still fresh. Help you get it out of your system."

"If that person on the trail set the fire, maybe I should have gone after them."

"And do what? Tackle them to the ground? You did exactly what you needed to by calling for help. And now, do this." Sheila reached into the canvas tote bag she carried to the store every day. She fished around until she found a notepad embossed with the logo of a publishing company whose books she carried. "Write it down. I'm going to head in and open up the store. I'll see you later?"

Penny nodded and rolled a pen between her fingers as Sheila closed her bag and left the warmth of the kitchen, stepping out into the cool winter air that Penny had just left. But she hadn't yet shaken off her chill.

She wrote a quick version of the events of the morning. Even after retelling them, her memories were crystallizing around the image of Jacob, leaning over the motionless woman, rhythmically thrusting his clutched palms into her ribcage. She saw him still as a teenage boy, the junior firefighter who'd skip classes to polish the fire trucks and sweep the apparatus bay until Chief Pintz got a call from the school principal, who knew exactly where Jacob would be.

But he grew up, Penny thought as she pushed herself away from the table and headed for the bathroom to take a hot shower. And she had too. Seeing Jacob made her know she couldn't hide forever in a town like Shells Harbour.

The soap and water warmed her chilled skin and cleaned away the last of the smell of smoke from her hair. She forced thoughts of Jacob and the fire from her mind and began planning her day.

Penny had worked in publishing in Toronto, marketing new books by famous authors she rarely met. She had been hoping to work her way up to be an editor in the conglomerate that had swallowed up smaller rivals along its way to being one of the biggest publishers in Canada. But the corporate world ground her down. And her relationship with Callum unraveled. Not when the last harsh word was said on another late night of suspicion, of waiting until he fell asleep to peek at his phone and have her suspicions confirmed. Her relationship crumbled and her career was on ice. She put Toronto city limits in her rear-view mirror and headed for the only home she thought she had left.

Penny minded the counter through the quiet winter afternoons at Brittle Pages to give Sheila a break and feel like she was earning her keep after her aunt took her in. She had leveraged a few industry connections to get some freelance marketing work with smaller publishing houses to keep a bit of cash coming in. She'd soothed the sore spot in her heart that Callum had left, ignoring his calls and e-mails apart from one last note to let him know they were done.

Penny dried off and slipped into jeans, a t-shirt and warm socks. She made a fresh pot of coffee and put some slices of bread in the toaster as she tried to focus on the work she needed to get done before heading to the bookstore.

Instead, she glanced at the screen of her phone. It showed a notification for a new message that had come in while she was in the shower.

I didn't know you were in town. I need to talk to you. Jacob.

The coffee burbled, and the toast popped. But Penny stood in the centre of Sheila's kitchen, frozen to the spot. She knew Jacob had seen her and that eventually, she'd have to talk to him. She wondered if it was about the fire, or about her appearance back in town. Or something else entirely. She forced her fingers to type out a reply.

Four

The chime over the door at Brittle Pages tinkled and Sheila appeared from behind a stack of historical nonfiction. Penny's aunt still had the brightly coloured African print wrap tied around her hair.

"That does look lovely," Penny said. She was grateful for a splash of colour on the day that had become grey and dull. Penny set her cup of organic coffee from the Jungle Cafe down on the sales counter cluttered with giveaway bookmarks and brochures for Shells Harbour businesses.

Sheila patted the wrap. "Took me about four tries, but I saw Esi this morning and she approved."

Penny moved behind the counter and curled her hands around her cup of coffee. She was hoping for a quiet shift at the bookstore. She felt Sheila's eyes on her as she stared at the brown lid.

"You're still thinking about the fire."

Penny let a breath loose that she was holding in. She nodded. "I got nothing done on the copy I need to write for the agency in Toronto."

"That's understandable. You had a major shock."

"And you were right about an investigation. I'm glad you made me write what I saw."

"Who's investigating?"

"I'm not sure," Penny said.

"Is it the fire department? Did Paul call you?"

The tone in Sheila's voice made Penny glance up and saw a smile teasing the lines around her eyes. Sheila patted the scarf on her head and made a millimetre of an adjustment.

"How exactly do you know the deputy chief?"

"Oh yes. Paul and I went to school together," Sheila said. She turned back toward the non-fiction section she had been tidying before Penny came in.

"Right, he mentioned something about that," Penny said, grinning. Sheila had taken her mind off the fire for a moment.

"You spoke with Paul about me?"

Penny couldn't see her face and instead tried to decipher her voice. There was a hint of anxiety in Sheila's voice, or anticipation.

"Deputy Chief Haines knew my name right away. Because of Grandpa, as his first fire chief. And you too," Penny said, relishing her aunt's fluster.

"Well, we might have dated a bit. Went to a few dances together. But then I went to the city for university and he stayed here and got married. And that was that."

"You got married too. Did you forget?"

"You know, sometimes I do. Best thing I got from those two years was his last name. I love alliteration." Sheila dragged her name between the slight gap in her front teeth. "Sshheila Ssssutherland."

"Paul definitely hasn't forgotten you," Penny said. "Before they called for the rescue in the house, we chatted and he reminded me of the great Brittle Pages toaster fire."

"Oh, dear lord," Sheila said. "I was so embarrassed when he came here with the sirens all blaring and the lights flashing. Half of the town lined up outside, trying to get a peek in to see what I had done."

Penny scoffed. "That would stand to reason. No one has anything else to do with their time in this town other than talk about people."

"Well, that's a bit of an exaggeration, Pen," Sheila said.

"Is it though? Gossip ruins lives and people just say whatever they want. And no one gets held accountable."

Sheila paused for a moment, and Penny saw the smile lines around her aunt's eyes fade. Penny was uncertain where her outburst came from, but she'd never been good about hiding her feelings about Shells Harbour. She was born and raised in the town, but knew she never fully belonged.

"Jeez girl, it's been great having you back, but you need to get over this notion that we're any different here than anywhere else. Even up in your big city there. I bet lots of people went talking about you after you left that job of yours. Shells Harbour's no different from any other and you might want to think about letting go of some of the things that drove you away. Gossip happens everywhere, and it only ruins lives if you let it."

Sheila had emerged from behind a bookshelf to deliver her response to Penny, looking her straight in the eyes as she did.

Penny had trouble maintaining Sheila's stare. She had a point, but she doubted that her former coworkers in Toronto spent much time pondering her empty desk on the first Monday she didn't show up. She preferred it that way.

Shells Harbour had been toxic for her as a teenager, grating against her skin like the raw ocean wind in a storm, swirling until she fled for Toronto. But when she needed a place to run, Shells Harbour was it. After being back for three months, Penny felt the cloak of her purposeful anonymity being tugged away.

"Jacob is investigating the fire," Penny said. "Jacob Bell. We went to school together."

Sheila nodded. "I heard he was the town fire director now," she said, allowing Penny's quick subject change to float by. "I'm sure he'll just have a few questions for you. Have you spoken to him since you've been back?"

Penny shook her head, though she suspected her aunt knew the answer. Sheila was aware of Penny's reluctance to show her face around town. Sheila cleared her throat and gathered her oversized purse and tote bags laden with books she would read and decide on selling in her shop. Sheila found something to love in nearly all books she read, so the small shop would soon have a little more clutter.

"So, what do you need me to do today?"

"Biographies, if you don't mind. We've gotten a shipment from that publisher in the city. Some are local stories, so let's keep those out front."

"Is Esi meeting you here or at the market?"

The door chime tinkled the sound of an arrival and Esi Gyan swished in, a basket in the crook of her right arm and a thick cable-knit sweater pulled over a bright dress.

"Es, you look like you're about to drop anchor on a lobster boat. All you need is a ratty old Sou'wester," Sheila laughed.

"A what?"

"This," Penny said, pointing to a book on the Local Lore shelf that featured a wrinkled fisherman on the cover with the floppy yellow hat.

"Well, I finally got Sheila wearing something African on her head. I guess I can try something Canadian," Esi said.

"Come on, let's get to the market before Erin Riggings gets all the fresh eggs again," Sheila said, grabbing her basket and her friend's free arm. Penny watched as they crossed Barque Lane and headed up the cracked sidewalk for the short walk to the weekly market in the lobby of the spacious town hall. The restored heritage building was one of the most photographed buildings in Shells Harbour. Its Gothic style prompted legends of hauntings and spooky encounters.

She switched on the radio and listened to the local station, but there was no news yet of the fire. The weather update gave way to fiddle and folk tunes that made a good pace for working. She sipped her coffee and surveyed the cardboard box of books in a corner that would be her task for the next few hours.

Penny glanced around for a cutter to slit open the layer of packing tape that sealed the box. Seeing none in the jumble of the shop's sales counter, she slid past the stacks and went into the small back-room kitchen.

Penny pulled hard on the handle of a stiff wooden drawer, heaving with a might she didn't quite realize she had. All the contents — spoons, bent forks, rusted knives — clattered to the linoleum floor. Penny cursed and leaned over to root through the contents until she found a pointed knife that looked sharp enough to slice the tape.

"Are you alright?"

Penny stood up and whipped around at the male voice. She gripped the knife tighter and held it in front of her as she met Jacob Bell's blue-eyed gaze.

Five

"Woah, woah, Penny," Jacob said, a nervous smile edging his mouth. "Sorry if I scared you. I heard a noise when I came in."

Penny quickly dropped the blade to her side and laughed.

"Oh God, Jacob, no. I just pulled the drawer out. I didn't hear you come in."

"Are you okay, though?"

"Yes, yes, I'm fine. Just making a bit of a mess."

He leaned toward her and pulled the wooden drawer up off the floor. With a bit of force, he replaced it in the cupboard.

"Thanks," Penny said as she dumped a handful of knives and spoons into the drawer. He was close enough that she could smell a faint covering of smoke on his jacket. In high school, she remembered, he smelled like sporty deodorant and the cheap cologne boys doused over their clothes. But that, like so many other things, had changed as they grew up.

Penny had answered Jacob's text earlier and told him she would be at the bookstore to answer any questions he had about the fire. And now he stood in front of her, the picture of her past, with a warmer smile than she deserved for leaving their friendship behind without so much as a backward glance.

Penny moved around Jacob to lead them from the cramped kitchen back into the store. She laid the knife on the cash counter between them to use later on the box of books she needed to shelve.

"How long have you been back in Shells Harbour?"

"Since Christmas, actually," Penny said. She was aching to sound casual, to refer to the hardest decision of her life in a calm, measured tone. As if upending her life was no big deal.

She looked at Jacob's face closely for the first time since he came in. He had a slight shadow of a dark beard and his brown hair spiked at the ends from the ribbed toque he'd pulled off his head. His broad shoulders offset a hint of a paunch that had appeared in the years since high school, although it was somewhat enhanced by the belt he had cinched around his pants. Which, Penny noticed, seemed to be part of a uniform. As was his shirt and jacket. Navy blue with a logo on the breast.

"You were still in Toronto?"

"Yep." Penny offered nothing else. After a beat, Jacob filled the silence.

"It's nice to have you back, Peepee." Penny rolled her eyes. But the mention of the high school nickname he had for her eased the divide of time between them. Still, she offered a slight smile, and Jacob laughed. "Sorry. Couldn't help myself."

Penny softened and perched herself on the wooden stool Sheila kept behind the sales counter.

"I'm sorry I didn't get in touch," she said. "I'm still a little, well, uncertain about being back."

"I can see that. Are you here for good, though?"

Penny didn't know the answer, because she wasn't sure herself. She'd enjoyed being close with Sheila again. But questions about her place in the town played on her mind. After a few months back, a restlessness was creeping in, along with silent questions about her career, her future. She was 32, and she was starting over. Penny realized Jacob was looking at her, waiting for an answer.

"To be honest with you, I'm not sure. But I'm here now, and it's nice to be able to help Sheila again."

He glanced around, taking in Brittle Pages' full shelves. "I remember visiting you here after school while you were working," he said. "Just like old times."

"And I remember you skipping class to go to the fire hall. So, I guess that hasn't changed either."

Jacob laughed. He moved toward the children's section and selected a graphic novel by a Halifax writer. "You think this would be okay for a seven-year-old? My son loves comic books, but I'd like him to try a bit more of a challenge."

Penny's eyes widened. She brought her hands to her cheeks, which were still warm from her fluster in the kitchen.

"You're a dad?"

He nodded and smiled.

"I can't believe I didn't know that."

"Well, there's a lot we don't know about each other anymore. He's seven, like I said, going on 17. Growing up way too fast. Do you have any?"

Penny shook her head. She'd been with Callum for close to five years and there was a time she would have loved nothing more than to be a mother to his children. To build a life with him and have a family. But the last year of their relationship had been a series of lies, each thicker than the last. Jacob didn't need to know any of that, though.

"I'd love to meet your son someday."

"I'm sure you will. He's with his mom this week. You remember Jess? She was a year behind us in school."

Penny nodded. Jacob and Jess Anderson started dating in high school, becoming joined at the hip in Penny and Jacob's senior year. But Jacob's description of Chris being with Jess for the week let Penny know she wasn't the only one with a breakup story. It was too soon to ask Jacob for the details, but down the road, that could come. She was already warming to the idea of having their friendship back.

Until Jacob glanced around the other shelves. Penny sensed immediately that he had turned serious. There was no more talk of kids or old nicknames.

"Sheila's not here, is she?"

"No, why?"

"No other customers? No one in the back?" Penny shook her head and pinched her fingers into fists under the counter, nervous. Jacob leaned closer, crossing the open space over the cash desk between them.

"Was a damn surprise seeing you at the fire. Thought I was imagining it."

"I just wish I had gotten there sooner," Penny said, although she felt as if Jacob had something more to say. She tried to stop herself from carrying on like she did on her call with the emergency operator. Her nervous habit. So often, she'd chat endlessly to Callum about the weather forecast or what happened on the streetcar that morning to avoid having serious conversations as their relationship unravelled. "I wish I had called 9-1-1 faster or done something else. Can I ask, how is the woman?"

Jacob ran a hand through his brown hair and looked at her. Penny saw the lines that were starting to settle around his eyes, the edge of unease that clouded the blue. He shook his head.

"That's what I wanted to talk to you about. In person, not over the phone. We tried. I worked on her for a few minutes, trying to get her heart restarted, get her breathing. The other guys stepped in. The paramedics tried to revive her, but she didn't make it."

Penny brought her hand to her mouth and her worry about not calling for help soon enough pivoted to sadness for Jacob. "I'm so sorry," she said. He let out some air and turned away. The space that felt close between them was now a gulf and she wanted to console her old friend. But the years that had passed had taken away any right Penny had to comfort him.

He stepped toward the picture window that looked out onto Barque Lane. Penny struggled to decipher his body language. Their friendship had never been romantic when they were in high school, but there was a time that she could tell nearly everything about Jacob. From the way he would cock his head to the side when he listened to a question in math class, or the way he'd rub his fingers through his hair when he was worried, like he did just before he spoke.

Now, she could only look at him as he stared through the window

Sheila had cluttered with posters for new releases and a display of books that changed every month.

"I've lost several people since I became a firefighter. Two car accidents. Too many that we can't revive on medical calls. Heart attacks. But this is the first one in a fire. We don't see it much around here."

"But you've seen it. And that's terrible."

Jacob turned back to face her. "It's a hard thing to deal with," he said. "And it's even harder when it's someone you know."

Penny felt her stomach muscles clench. She felt sick for Jacob.

"You knew her?"

He nodded.

"And so did you."

Six

Penny lifted another stack of books from one of Brittle Pages' dusty corners. It was a small shop, but there were endless nooks and crannies that hid Sheila's picks. Penny placed the stack on the sales counter, which held the shop's lone computer. She entered each title into Sheila's catalogue of books and sales.

The repetitive work helped as she settled into the rhythm of the afternoon. She hoped it would bring calm and quiet. And a chance to absorb Jacob's news.

The late winter sun emerged from the morning cloud to warm the picture window with its display of books. Sheila had added hand-painted flowers in an optimistic call ahead to spring. Penny tried to focus on cataloging the stack of gardening memoirs, books with smiling ladies on the covers, wearing flowered gloves and straw hats, surrounded by blossoms. The doorbell chimed and a plump woman with long, grey hair spilling over the collar of a pink quilted jacket rushed in. Her presence immediately took over the shop.

"Good afternoon, ma'am, how are you today?" Penny greeted the woman with a formality that she tried to tinge with friendliness. She was grateful for the appearance of a customer. A distraction.

"Oh, I suppose I'm alright. You're Penny, right? Sheila's niece? Back from Toronto."

"Yes, that's me," Penny replied warily. She realized the woman in front of her wasn't a passing-by shopper.

"It's just awful about that big fire at old Coleridge's place there in the woods," the woman said, her brown eyes trained on Penny.

"Oh, yes," she muttered, unsure. Jacob had asked her to keep silent the news about the woman found in the fire and she was certain to honour that. "Is there something I can help you with today? We have some lovely new books to help you get the garden ready for spring." Penny held up the top title on her stack, a woman kneeling among vines of ripe tomatoes and beans.

The woman shook her head. "Look at those tomatoes. Last year was terrible for them. No, until someone finds it thrilling enough to write about turnips and cabbage, which is about the only thing we can count on growing around here, I am done with those books."

Penny forced a smile at the woman, who still hadn't introduced herself. Shells Harbour residents treated each other with a friendly ease, but Penny's guard was up.

"You know who had a lovely garden?" The woman carried on before giving Penny a chance to guess. "Coleridge Coleman. For a time he did, anyway. Grew some lovely vegetables and had a table at the farmer's market. He'd sell out every week. He hasn't done that in a few years, though. Poor man just never quite fit in around here and might not have the chance now."

The woman brought her gloved hand to her mouth and turned away to face a rack of crime novels. Penny couldn't tell if the reaction was a genuine gesture of concern or sadness. Her words seemed tinged with a question she hadn't yet asked. Penny didn't respond. After a long moment, the woman pulled a book off the shelf and began running her finger along the back cover.

"You must have been rather quick in getting there. Are you quite a fast runner?"

Penny narrowed her eyebrows and looked at the woman. Outside of the firefighters, Sheila was the only person who knew Penny was at the scene of the blaze.

The door chimed again. Penny was relieved to see Sheila and Esi come in, laden with baskets from the market. When Sheila saw the woman in the pink coat, her face hardened.

"Well Erin, now I know why we didn't see you at the market. Here you are. How are you today?"

Penny mulled over the name. Erin. It rang no bells for her.

"Hello Sheila. It's hard to think about something as trivial as shopping on a tragic day like today," Erin said. "I wanted to come here and check on your poor niece. I'm surprised you left her alone, after what she's been through."

"Oh, how kind of you," Sheila said. But Penny knew her aunt's tone was telling another story, a cautionary one where the woman called Erin was being warned. Penny had heard it herself plenty of times. Step lightly, it said. "I think she'll be quite alright, though."

"I need to get back to my shop," Esi said. She had a store a few streets over where she offered travel agency services and bookkeeping for small businesses. "Why don't I walk you out, Erin?"

Esi nodded to Sheila and opened the door to the shop. Erin looked between the women.

"Fine," she said, turning to Penny. "But if you need to talk about what happened, dear, I'm here for you." She swept out the door without waiting for Esi.

Penny turned back to her aunt. "Do I know her? She certainly seemed to know me."

"Well, if you don't yet, you will soon. Everyone in this town knows her. You either run away from her when you see her coming, or toward her. Erin Riggings will become your best friend if you've got gossip, or an ear to listen to it."

"Sometimes she even gets it right," Esi said, shifting her basket of vegetables on her arm. "But you never quite know what to believe with her."

"She doesn't hold back, does she?" Penny asked. She shared her aunt's sensibility and honed her instinct for people in the years she watched Sheila deal with customers behind the counter of Brittle Pages.

"Your aunt and Mrs. Riggings have little love lost between them,"

Esi said with a laugh. "One ill-fated season with both of them trying to organize the ice sculpture competition at the Winter Carnival."

Sheila groaned. "That's what I get for volunteering. It all ended in a giant puddle of melted ice, some very upset carvers and a company sponsor who has never given another cent to the carnival."

"I just don't get how she knew I was at the fire," Penny said. "It's only been a few hours since it happened."

"Someone recognized you," Sheila said simply, as if it was entirely expected that Penny would be talked about. "One of the other fire-fighters, probably."

Penny went back to her perch behind the counter. Erin Riggings' visit made Shells Harbour feel like a fist tightening its grip. She could feel pressure in her chest.

There was another time in Penny's life when she worked behind the counter at Brittle Pages, and people like Erin would slide into the shop. Back then, they were sniffing around for gossip about Penny's mother, Delphine, the subject of town talk for a few months in Penny's sopho-more year of high school. Sheila told her to ignore them, but being the daughter of Delphine Pintz played on Penny's teenage mind and left long shadows that stretched more than a decade later.

"Who's Coleridge Coleman?" Penny asked, forcing her thoughts back to the present. "That's a weird name."

"Weird name for a weird guy. He owns the mobile home where the fire was this morning," Sheila answered.

"He's eccentric," Esi said. "A collector of odd things. He keeps to himself other than when he's rambling about the countryside, adding to his collections."

"That explains some of the junk I saw in his yard," Penny said. "Stuff everywhere."

With a gush of cold outdoor air, Erin Riggings came back inside Brittle Pages. Penny shivered.

"Well, I thought you all would like to know, I didn't get ten feet up the road when I ran into Mrs. Martin who heard from her niece that there was a police car this morning in front of Dr. Truitt's house."

Penny kept silent. She knew it wouldn't be long now before the quiet that Jacob asked her to keep would come out.

"They clearly weren't doing a traffic stop, so I figure it has something to do with the body Penny found," she said.

"I didn't find it," Penny said.

"Mrs. Martin's niece said she read online that Mrs. Truitt wasn't at hockey practice last night. Did you see her there, Esi? Doesn't your young fella play on the same team as hers?"

"Yes, but not every parent goes to every hockey practice. I don't. That rink's too cold for me."

"Vicki Truitt did, I bet. She did everything. We're on the Winter Carnival committee with her," Erin said, gesturing to Esi.

At the mention of the name, Penny exhaled sharply enough to catch the other women's attention.

"Oh my word, it was Vicki, wasn't it?"

Penny looked at Erin with a glance that couldn't hide her distaste for the woman she'd just met. She slid off the stool from behind the counter and moved toward the kitchen. "I'm going to make some tea."

She wouldn't be the one to confirm what Jacob had told her earlier. He'd asked her to keep silent, even knowing that the town's rumour mill would churn out speculation until it was satisfied with an answer. He wanted to buy a bit of time to gather facts, but that time was now up.

Esi poked her head into the kitchen. "She's gone now. You're safe."

"Am I, though? Isn't this how it starts?"

Esi was silent for a moment. "I'd like to say that people like Erin are harmless, but I'm not sure I can. She really shouldn't be running around here, fishing for information about Vicki Truitt. The woman was a wife and a mother, for goodness sake. Her children might not even know."

"You know her sister, Pen. Arlene. She married a Tanner, but she was a Lowery when you were friends."

"I called her Leenie. And I was Peepee."

Penny had a flash of her friend, and Saturday nights in Leenie's old Pontiac Sunfire, driving the curving roads around Shells Harbour, visiting friends' houses and collecting enough people to get a bonfire together at the gravel pit outside town. Jacob and his girlfriend would be there, arms wrapped around each other, and sometimes if they were feeling generous, Leenie and Peepee would let Vicki tag along.

Penny remembered Arlene's little sister as a bit of a pest, anxious about being included, sitting on the edge of the bonfires as if she was afraid to be noticed, but even more afraid to not "Two more years Vic, and you can get out of here," Penny told the younger girl once, just before leaving for university. "Just like us."

But Vicki wouldn't get out unscathed. Not from high school, thanks to Penny's own mother, as she found out not long after graduation. And now, Vicki would never leave Shells Harbour.

Seven

Penny turned up the heat in her red Volkswagen. The car idled, and the heater sent out a stronger current of warmth against the chill that had settled over Shells Harbour. The afternoon was about to give way to the evening and the residential street had an early sunset orange tinge. She glanced at the dust on the dash, at the display on the radio station that quietly warbled out a light pop song. She reached up to press the knob, turning it off.

Penny had driven by the house twice, just to make sure. Shells Harbour was one of the last few villages in rural Nova Scotia where houses still had individual mailboxes, rather than anonymous slots at a central location like a corner store or church. She was certain she had the right house. The Tanner name was on the mailbox, Arlene and Zachary. And a discoloured spot where another name might once have been.

Leenie Lowery and Peepee Pintz had been attached at the hip through junior and senior high school. They spent long hours listening to pop music, playing with makeup, and writing letters that were passed underneath textbooks in class. As they grew older, Penny would visit Arlene late in the evening at her job at the local gas station, and the girls took cigarettes an underage Arlene bought before the station installed security cameras. They'd sneak outside for smoke breaks that never lasted more than a few puffs until the girls were coughing and laughing.

Penny told Arlene everything. Almost everything, Penny had to admit to herself as the Volkswagen idled. They knew every crush and shared all their secrets, except for one that sat like a rock in Penny's stomach until she left Shells Harbour. It was the one that kept Penny away from her best friend for years.

Until now. With a deep breath in and out, Penny unbuckled her seat belt and opened the car door, reaching back in for the lattes she picked up at the Jungle Cafe. She hoped Arlene still drank them like they did on their Saturday shopping trips to Halifax, when they'd watch sophisticated city people from a window perch at the Second Cup coffee shop downtown. They had a confidence and swagger rural Shells Harbour couldn't match, Penny thought then, wishing she could be one of them.

She glanced around. Arlene's neighbourhood was on the newer side of Shells Harbour. Homes there were built in the 1960s and 70s rather than the turn of the century, when the fishing industry boom brought new families to the old town. The houses were built close together, but not so close as to feel intrusive. Many of them, like Arlene's, had small, sloping lawns that were dried and patchy and would soon be snow-covered before becoming full with spring growth. Penny looked up at the sky, high and white. The forecast was promising snow after sunset.

Penny balanced the latte cups on top of each other and pressed the doorbell at the front of the bungalow.

The white door swung open, revealing a grim-faced pre-teen boy.

"Can I help you?" His voice was a rasp on the cusp of belonging to a man. Penny recognized him from Arlene's online photos as her son, Zachary. He was taller than Penny thought he'd be. But then, she hadn't seen him since he was a preschooler, when Penny ran into Arlene and the child at the grocery store on a rare visit home. That encounter had been excruciating for Penny. She wanted to melt into the produce displays as she made awkward small talk with Arlene and was relieved when Zach fussed enough to prompt her to say good-bye to Penny.

"Hey Zach, is your Mom home?"

Zach didn't seem puzzled by a strange woman at his door. Although Penny guessed she wouldn't have been the first surprise visitor of the day at the Tanner house, as word about Vicki's death spread.

Before the boy summoned his mother, she appeared behind him.

"Well, look what the cat dragged in," Arlene said.

Penny found herself lost for words. Arlene's hazel eyes were puffed and red. She ached for not getting in touch with her old friend sooner and the weight of her departure after high school still hung over them. But Penny immediately knew it wasn't the time to have the deep conversation their friendship needed.

Instead of offering words, Penny offered a latte as Zach wandered back into the home.

"I've been getting phone calls all morning, when this is the only thing I really wanted. Couldn't get out of the house long enough to get to the Jungle, not that I wanted to see anybody," Arlene said. "It's good to see you, though. I knew you were back in town."

"You did? Well, I guess I'm not surprised about that."

Arlene ushered Penny inside and led her toward the kitchen. Penny glanced at the walls. Framed school photos showed Zach through the years, smiling gap-toothed grins that seemed far from the young man who'd opened the door to Penny. There was Zach in a blue and white hockey uniform, in a mock-up of a sports card. It listed his date of birth, and Penny quickly did the math. Zach was 12. Which means Penny had last seen Arlene when they were 22. A decade had passed between the friends.

Penny noticed the absence of something, too. Pictures of Tim, Arlene's husband, had disappeared from her social media and he wasn't on the walls of the family home.

Arlene entered a sunny yellow and white kitchen. Notices and school assignments covered a stainless-steel refrigerator. Mugs, canisters and a bowl of browning bananas cluttered the counter. There was an island in the middle with a few bar-style stools and Arlene offered Penny one.

She was relieved that Arlene felt no inclination to have a stilted reunion in a family room, but rather carried on the unspoken tradition of generations of Shells Harbour women. The kitchen was where families and friends gathered to drink tea and wine and share their lives.

It was where they gathered for gossip and news. And where they came together in grief and mourning.

"Arlene, I'm so sorry about Vicki. I just can't believe it."

Arlene ran a thin hand through hair that was showing hints of emerging grey. The women were the same age, with birthdays separated by just a few months. But the strains of whatever she had been facing in life had added extra years to Arlene's appearance. Her cheekbones were sharp. The softness of their teenage years had hardened with time.

"I still can't really understand it, to be honest. It makes no sense."

"It's impossible to understand," Penny said, searching for platitudes to console Arlene. "She was so young."

Arlene paused, taking a full sip of her latte.

"I mean, I don't understand why she was there. At the trailer."

Penny had wondered how much Arlene knew about her sister's death. A lot of information had gone around in a short time, floating through the air in the town's gathering spots like the front counter at Brittle Pages or the back tables of the Jungle Cafe.

"Did she know Coleridge Coleman?"

Arlene let out a short laugh. "My sister wouldn't have associated with someone like him. Don't get me wrong, I don't have any feelings about Coleridge one way or the other. He always nodded at me when I'd see him at the grocery store and he used to split wood for my grandfather. He'd go over to Grandpa's land when the wood got delivered, junk it up and stack it. 'Ol Bertie pays me right good,' he'd say." Arlene smiled.

"Oh yeah? He paid him a lot?"

"Not in cash. He'd give Coleman whatever junk he had laying around and a bottle of rum."

Penny offered a smile and put the thought of discussing anything other than Vicki's death firmly out of her mind. Arlene had welcomed her into her home, acting like the years and time hadn't swept a decade between them. Penny wouldn't add to her grief and pain by dredging up the past. Not now.

Instead, she took a measured breath and thought about how she should phrase the words she was about to say. Arlene sipped her drink and looked back at Penny, waiting, as if she knew her old friend had something to tell her.

"Arlene, I don't know if you've heard. But I was there. At the fire."

"What do you mean?"

"I was on the trail. Getting a run in. It was a really nice day, you know, for February. The sun was out, and it wasn't too cold and I hadn't gone for a run in a while." Penny cringed at her babbling, but Arlene was patient.

"Go on, Penny."

Penny glanced around Arlene's kitchen. A hint of a garlicky dinner still hung in the air, maybe a lasagna or spaghetti a neighbour had made and dropped off for the family now in mourning. In the sink, dishes waited to be washed and a loaf of bread with half the slices eaten rested against a toaster. The kitchen was warm. Lived in. A sanctuary for Arlene and Zach that was punctuated now with grief.

"I didn't know where I was, but I just knew I smelled smoke. And it wasn't wood smoke, like someone's stove going," Penny said. "It was plastic. Chemical, almost. And then I saw him. Or her."

"Vicki?" Arlene's eyes widened.

"No, no, not your sister. I don't know who it was. Someone jumped out on the tracks ahead of me. Had a black hoodie up over their head. I think it might have been a man, or a woman with narrow hips, maybe. But kind of tall. And they moved fast."

"You have no idea who it was?"

Penny shook her head. "They didn't stop for a second. Could have been anybody, Leenie," she said, taking a chance on using her friend's old nickname.

"That's one I haven't heard in a long time." Arlene smiled, although the expression didn't touch her reddened eyes.

Penny continued to tell Arlene about following the smell through the rough trail in the woods that led to Coleman's cluttered yard. She told her about the heavy, thick smoke, peeling with abandon from the window of the mobile home. Her call to 9-1-1.

Penny left out the part where the operator asked if anyone was inside.

"And then the fire department showed up," Penny said.

Arlene had been frozen with attention through Penny's story. Whatever she was feeling, it wasn't numbness. Arlene was alert.

"Pen, were you there when they found her?"

"Yes, I was," Penny said. She wanted to give Arlene the truth. "I didn't know it was Vicki, but I watched the firefighters try to save her. Jacob tried to save her."

"Jacob Bell?"

"Yeah, he's in the fire department. And he's the town fire director, so he's going to be investigating," Penny said. "We've already spoken, so he knows everything I'm telling you. But I wanted you to hear it from me."

"They tried to save her," Arlene said to herself, her voice trailing. Her energy seemed to fade. Arlene turned her gaze out the window, to where Zach was shooting a hockey puck into a net in the driveway. A light snow fell.

"We fought," Arlene said, returning her attention to Penny. "A lot."

Penny stayed silent, watching her old friend.

"She was my sister. I loved her, but we weren't close. Not anymore. These last few years, she was different."

"How so?"

"Vicki's son, Jared, is just a year younger than Zach and they were as close as brothers when they were little. But as the boys got older, Vicki got really into everything they did. It wasn't enough just to go to the hockey games. Vicki was there in every last way, organizing everything and telling the parents what to do. People would ask me to get her to back off, but they didn't know we just didn't have that kind of relationship anymore."

"I remember how close you were in high school. She'd follow you everywhere."

"I barely recognized her anymore, to be honest with you. In the last few years, we hardly ever spoke and if we did, it was a fight."

"What did you fight about?"

"Everything. She'd fight about what colours the new jerseys for the hockey team should be. Last summer, she coached baseball and some kids quit the team because she was so mean to them. And you remember, our grandmother, Mary?"

Penny nodded.

"She's been over in Lazy Pines for a few years now. Vicki was obsessed these last few months with selling their house, the old place on Outcrop. I wanted to let Gram decide. But Vicki said we should strike while the iron was hot. Houses have been selling for a lot of money lately, especially anything near the ocean like Gram's house."

Penny thought about Mary Barkson, who would be in her late eighties now. On countless afternoons, Penny took the bus after school with Arlene and Vicki to the Barksons' house along the rocky edge of the Atlantic coast and rambled in the woods or explored the nooks and crannies of the home and the property.

The idea of the sisters being in a war was hard for Penny to imagine. For so much of their youth, Vicki was on Arlene's tail. Penny's memory of her was that of an eager young teenager. She would tie her blond hair in a ponytail that bounced around as she ran after Penny and Arlene. She wanted to read the same books the older girls read, watch the same shows on television, wear the same cheap drug store perfume.

Until the summer before Penny and Arlene's senior year in high school, and Vicki's sophomore grade, when a rumour spread about Vicki being involved with the owner of the pizza restaurant she worked at. It was untrue, but Penny watched Vicki mature rapidly from a girl with a bouncing ponytail and bright laugh to a young woman who had come to realize there was a darkness in people. And in the town.

That rumour followed Vicki around for months and lived like a shadow at the edges of Penny's quietest moments, even after she left Shells Harbour. Because she knew exactly how it started, and why.

"The service will be on Thursday. Roger's handling the details. Her husband."

Penny nodded.

Arlene paused. The snow was still lightly falling, loose flakes that hinted at worse to come. Zach shot his hockey pucks, each sending a soft thunk in the net.

Arlene pointed to a bouquet of red carnations mixed with white buds of baby's breath nestled in a vase on the kitchen table.

"My ex dropped those off," she said, and Penny let the words settle over her. "I don't know if you remember Tim. He works at Mariner's Sawmill now. We broke up a few months ago."

"I'm sorry to hear that, Arlene."

The woman was quiet. She reached out to touch one of the budding flowers and Penny almost winced as Arlene used her long fingernails to pinch off the head.

"He was an ass. But the sawmill is right next to Coleridge's house. Tim told me he'd seen Coleridge coming and going a lot lately."

"What do you think that means?"

"I don't know. Everyone knows Coleridge likes to wander, looking for junk that he scraps and sells. Tim was probably just looking for a reason to nose into his sister-in-law's death. Ex sister-in-law, although our divorce hasn't been finalized yet. I guess Vicki will take over from my divorce as the town's hot topic."

"You might be right," Penny said, but her thoughts had wandered from Arlene's kitchen to the memory of the person she'd seen on the trail behind Coleridge Coleman's burning home. Arlene flicked the head of the carnation she'd popped into her compost bin and turned back to Penny.

"I know how people talk around this town. They'll talk to everyone but the person who should be spoken to."

"That's true," Penny said.

"If you hear stuff about Vicki, will you tell me? I want to know. I need to know."

Penny nodded and stood up.

"Will you come on Thursday?"

"Of course, Leenie," Penny said with a smile.

"Thanks," Arlene said. But she couldn't return Penny's smile. "She was still my sister. I need to know what happened to her."

Eight

The storm from the night before left Shells Harbour under a layer of white. Banks of icy snow scraped up by plows grew against edges of the sidewalks where business owners were digging out their doorways. Penny opened the door to Brittle Pages and knocked off the snow that clung to the edges of her winter boots. The warmth of the bookstore, and the light smell of coffee from the pot that Sheila had brewing in the kitchen, helped her shake off the cold.

But she couldn't shake off Arlene's words from the day before. Arlene needed to find out what had happened to Vicki. And Penny, who was still trying to rid her mind of the image of Jacob trying to save Vicki's life, couldn't stop thinking about how Vicki Truitt ended up in Coleridge Coleman's trailer home.

"There's our girl," Sheila said, and Penny realized she wasn't the only person in the shop with her. Paul perched in an armchair near the front corner of the bookstore, a cozy nook that Sheila kept for customers who wanted a break from their browsing. And a place for visitors to stop for a chat. He wore a navy blue pullover with the clamshell logo of the Shells Harbour Fire Department embroidered on the chest and his name stitched into the left sleeve.

"I think I forgot how fickle our winters can be. It was only a few days ago that I was running on that bare trail." Penny said. "Hello, deputy chief."

"Call me Paul, please."

"Paul came by to see how you're getting on," Sheila said.

"Me? I suppose I'm alright," Penny moved further into the store and unzipped her winter coat. She kept quiet about the lingering sense that she should have done more. "Thank you for asking."

Penny lacked the small-town ease in how people related to each other in Shells Harbour, so she spoke to Paul Haines with a formality she used more often on strangers in Toronto who asked for directions or a waiter taking an order. Still, she saw the glance that Paul and Sheila exchanged, and she realized they were far from strangers.

"I should ask about you, though. And your firefighters. It must be a horrible thing to have to witness what they did."

Paul's greying eyebrows knotted, and he glanced away. Penny felt a wobble in her stomach for asking what had to have been an inappropriate question. The deputy chief cleared his throat.

"It's the worst thing we see on calls. Doesn't happen very much, thank goodness, but when it does, it's tough." Sheila crossed the few feet of space between them and put a hand on his shoulder.

"I'm terribly sorry. I shouldn't have asked," Penny said. But Paul shook his head.

"No, that's the old school way, I'm sorry to say, but that's the way of your grandfather and his generation."

"What do you mean?" Penny asked as she slid out of her bulky grey parka and hung it on a hook behind the door.

"Back in the day, if something bad happened on a call, something like what happened to the guys this week, we'd suck it up. Lot of them would drink it away. Couldn't talk about it cause we didn't even know we should. We're changing that now," he said.

"Suck it up. Yes, I heard that from my father more than once," Sheila said. "Suck it up and get back to it, he'd say, but then he'd go downstairs to his workshop in the basement for hours. He wouldn't come up for supper and he'd only come for the phone if it was one of the guys from the department calling. I asked him why once and he got angry and said no one else got it. No one else understood."

Paul nodded. "That's it. Your father was an excellent firefighter, he was a leader I model myself after. But I tell you, those old-school boys did it the hard way and you realize now that over time, we lost some of them who couldn't deal with the pain. So yes, my dear, you should have asked," he said, addressing the last part to Penny.

"Well then, if I may ask, how are you? And how are your firefighters?"

"They're doing alright, thank you. We're bringing in the counsellor tomorrow. That will be a big help because the guys that don't want to talk to each other usually will talk to her. She's a firefighter in a department down the coast, so she can relate."

"She? Are there many women in the fire service?"

Paul Haines laughed. "Certainly are. Another thing that's changed from back in the day. We have a few here in town. Excellent firefighters. You want an application?"

Penny looked from Paul to Sheila and felt her mouth gap open slightly as she searched for an answer. She pictured herself wearing that bulky gear like a beige snowsuit and even charging into a burning house. "I don't think so."

"You'd be surprised what you can do. Think about it."

Penny couldn't imagine keeping calm as flames surged around her. Or being the one who pulled a person from inside a burning building. And then trying to save their life. She needed to divert the topic.

"I went to see Arlene Tanner yesterday," she told Paul. "Vicki's sister. She wants to know what happened, and I didn't know what to say."

"Penny and Arlene were thick as thieves in high school," Sheila told Paul. "Couldn't find one without the other."

"I wanted her to hear from me that I had been at the fire," Penny said. "I told her Jacob and your firefighters tried their best."

Paul nodded. "They did, but I daresay it was a lost battle as soon as they found her."

Penny leaned on the counter and looked at the senior firefighter. If Vicki Truitt was already dead when they pulled her out, that might have meant Penny truly couldn't have helped her.

That doesn't really make me feel better, Penny thought, straightening a pile of brochures about the town's restaurants.

"Arlene doesn't understand what her sister was doing in Coleridge Coleman's trailer in the first place."

"They didn't know each other?" Sheila asked.

"Not according to Arlene. In fact, it sounds like Coleridge wasn't the type that her sister would associate with."

"I don't want to speak ill, but there was always something about Vicki," Paul said.

"You knew her?"

"Oh yes, your aunt knows this, but I was the administrator at the hospital before I took early retirement a few years ago. We had a board of directors who handled all sorts of affairs of the hospital and there's a committee of board and community members who ran the Winter Carnival, our biggest fundraiser of the year," Paul said.

Penny nodded. "Was the best thing about winter in Shells Harbour when I was a kid."

"I helped with the organizing for many years, but Vicki Truitt was on the committee and she got herself right involved. Took the whole thing over."

"The carnival's coming up soon, right?"

"Next week, but I don't know how they'll pull it off without her," Paul said. "Everything on the committee revolved around her. Although she wasn't making any friends, that's for sure."

"What do you mean?" Penny asked. She thought about Arlene's recounting of Vicki's intense involvement in her son's activities, and the pushback she'd gotten from other parents. Vicki's drive for control hadn't won her friends in Shells Harbour.

"I guess she just wanted to be in charge of pretty much everything. Especially the money. Every last thing that needed to be bought, she wanted to approve."

"Who else is on the committee?"

"Well, let's see. Her husband, Roger. Dr. Truitt. He was the last representative from the hospital who stayed on the committee. Not that he did much except show up and agree with Vicki."

"Who else?"

"Esi's on it," Sheila said. "She doesn't say much about it. When I used to ask her, she'd just roll her eyes and say that she had been taught that if you can't say anything nice, don't say anything at all." Penny glanced at Paul, who had a light smile dancing on his face, and nodded along with Sheila. "I stopped asking about it a couple of years ago," Sheila said. "Though I noticed last month that her name was on the committee list they printed in the newspaper."

"Do you still have the paper?" Penny asked.

"Oh probably. Should be in the kitchen," Sheila said.

"In the fire hazard, you mean," Penny said and Sheila let out a sharp laugh that brightened the bookstore. Penny saw Paul grin at Sheila's chuckle. She wondered whether he was reminiscing about their high school days or if he was thinking about something in the present when he looked at her aunt.

Penny went into the kitchen to dig up the paper and pour herself a cup of coffee. She idly listened to Paul and Sheila's chatter as she flipped through the pages. Their conversation drifted from the Winter Carnival to talk of the fire department, and other parts of their lives.

"About five, six years ago now," Penny heard Paul say. "We just, you know, grew apart. She was from Saskatchewan originally. Always wanted to go back and finally she went. By herself."

"Oh Paul, I'm sorry to hear that," Sheila said. Penny was now silent, eavesdropping closely. She could almost hear the shrug in his voice.

"It is what it is. I survived."

Penny made a show of crinkling the newspaper to let them know she was reemerging from the kitchen.

"Look at this. Here's the list. Yep, Vicki was chairperson, and there's Esi. And also," Penny paused and looked at her aunt. "Erin Riggings, deputy chair?"

"I think that's one of the reasons why Esi doesn't talk about the committee. It's a wonder they get anything done at all," Sheila said. Paul glanced at her with raised eyebrows. "Oh, you know Erin. Wears that puffy pink coat and zooms all over the market every week, chatting with every vendor who makes eye contact. She's married to Ward Riggings, who owns the sail shop over by the wharf."

Paul nodded. "Ah, yes. I know exactly who you mean. She complained to council about us going through town late one evening with the sirens on. Apparently, we made her miss the last few minutes of her show," he said, pulling the memory from what had to have been a deep file of Shells Harbour disasters. "We were responding to a house fire. We rescued a trapped dog in that one. Put the pooch right back in the arms of its owner."

Sheila shook her head, but to Penny, it sounded perfectly in line with some of the town residents she knew. She flipped the pages of the local paper that offered more ads for business than anything like current events. But news of a death would top the next edition.

"I need to pick up something to wear to Vicki's memorial. All my formal clothes went to Goodwill when I left Toronto."

"Not much need for fancy around here," Paul said.

"I needed to pack light, anyway."

A stillness settled over them for just a moment, until a monotone shriek from a radio clipped to Paul's belt shattered the calm.

"Oh, damn." He was no longer Paul, the Brittle Pages visitor and Sheila's old friend. He was Deputy Chief of the Shells Harbour Fire Department. The shriek gave way to a woman's voice, a dispatcher in an office somewhere who relayed 9-1-1 calls to the emergency responders, like the one Penny had made.

"Shells Harbour Fire Department, please respond to a vehicle on fire, close to civic address 222 Outcrop Road."

"Gotta go," Paul said, and tugged open the burgundy door, sending the bell into a clang.

Penny glanced at Sheila, who couldn't contain the smile spreading across her face as she gathered up the coffee cup she'd drained during Paul's visit.

"I think he likes you," Penny said.

"Shush."

Sheila was busy tying her long grey hair back up into its customary bun. She swept it like a cascade over her right shoulder when Paul was in Brittle Pages.

"I know you said Esi doesn't like to talk about Vicki and the Winter Carnival, but do you think she might talk to me about it?"

"I don't really know, Pen. But why are you interested in all this?"

Penny paused, running her fingers along a blue and white knit scarf she hadn't unwrapped from around her neck. She glanced at her aunt.

"Arlene was my best friend once, and she's hurting."

Sheila stayed quiet, waiting for her niece to continue.

"I left her a long time ago. I'm not going to leave her now. If I can help her find out what might have been going on with her sister, I will. I have to. She was there for me a long time ago, in ways that —"

"That I wasn't?"

"No, it's not like that. Not at all. You were always there for me, even when I didn't deserve you." Penny reached across the cluttered counter and put her hands on her aunt's. "You were the grownup I needed Mom to be. You're still my grownup."

Sheila smiled. "You staying with me is just as much for my benefit as it might be for you."

"It's hard to explain. I had you, and you were the adult I needed. But Arlene was my best friend. She was like family. And I threw her away when I threw away this whole town."

"You were 18. You had a great opportunity for school in Toronto."

"Still. When I saw Zach at the house yesterday, I realized I had only seen him once, when he was little. Just a toddler. She was a mother right out of college. And now she's doing it alone. She and Tim have separated."

"So, you want to find out what happened to her sister to get your best friend back?"

Penny smiled. Her aunt knew exactly how to cut to the chase with her.

"Something like that."

"Well, in that case, I'll give Esi a call and tell her you're on the way over."

Nine

Penny's boots crunched along the fresh snow on the sidewalk. The last flurries from the previous night's storm skittered through the air, leaving a light coating on cars and garbage bins. Shells Harbour looked pretty in the snow. Lights glowed inside warm, candy-coloured shops offering antique curios, hand-stitched aprons and folk art that delighted tourists in the summer months when the town's narrow lanes became busy hubs for visitors who wandered into traffic to snap pictures on their phones.

In the near distance, Penny heard the wailing sirens of fire trucks responding to the call that had chased Paul out of Sheila's shop so quickly. Penny smiled, tucking her chin into her scarf, when she thought about the way the pair had been. She didn't know what the history was between the two of them, but there was something about the way her aunt responded to him that gave Penny pause.

Esi's shop had become one of Penny's favourite places in Shells Harbour. She pulled the door open to a haven of warmth on the winter afternoon. Penny assumed Esi kept the heat up in part to remind herself of Ghana, the country she left behind, and to give potential travellers a taste of what might await them on the adventure they were coming to book through her agency.

"Hello my dear." Esi greeted Penny with a hug like a long unseen relative every time. That was her charm, one of the things that kept her business running even in an era of self-booking through online travel sites.

Penny was relieved that Esi still had warmth in her voice, even though she suspected Sheila had warned her that Penny was coming to discuss a subject Esi hadn't been eager to broach in the past. But that was before a death shadowed the Shells Harbour Winter Carnival.

"Hello Auntie Esi." Penny felt immediately at ease in the comfortable shop. In the few months since Penny had returned from Toronto, her aunt's friendship with Esi had delighted her. And Penny could quickly see that Esi's personality had brought out the best in her aunt. Sheila was never shy, but Penny knew her aunt could be reserved, even seem detached and uninterested. But it was survival in a town like Shells Harbour, where gossip was currency.

Esi poured a dollop of milk in a chipped mug with the logo of the Fighting Clams, the Shells Harbour High School cartoon mascot. She added in a flow of steaming orange pekoe tea warmed by a hot plate that was kept on a bookshelf lined with brochures for an assortment of Caribbean and African travel destinations.

"I put it on as soon as Sheila called me to say you were coming over." Esi smoothly poured the tea but didn't meet Penny's gaze when she slid the cup over. "I heard sirens just now. Did you hear them? I hope it's not another big one." Penny could tell she was distracted.

"It's a car fire, out on Outcrop Road." When Esi raised her eyebrows, Penny explained. "The deputy chief was in the bookshop when his pager went off."

"The deputy chief. You mean, Paul? Paul Haines?"

Penny nodded.

"Paul Haines was in Sheila's shop," Esi said, digesting the information with a slight nod. Penny wondered how much Esi might know about Paul, and his apparent fondness for her aunt.

"He claimed he was checking to make sure I was alright, but I think we both know it was more than a courtesy call," Penny said. She felt like a fisherman, casting a line far off the pier to see what would bite.

But Esi wouldn't be hooked that easily.

"Well, I don't know much about it. He certainly seems like a nice man, so it wouldn't be out of character for him to be concerned about you," Esi said.

She probably wants to hear this all from Sheila before saying anything to me about it, and I should stop spreading gossip, Penny thought as she gingerly touched the hot mug of tea. She allowed the subject to change as Esi poured her own cup and took a sip.

"And are you fine?"

"I am. I'm just worried about Arlene. Vicki's sister. She's upset, of course, and wants answers."

Esi nodded. "That's when we drink tea. Here in Canada, I put cold milk in. Back home, we used a little can of milk. I loved taking the opener, cracking it into the can, and serving it to my grandmother when she would visit from the village. She was very formal, and everything would have to be arranged neatly on the tray."

Penny relished Esi's stories from Ghana and knew that talking about it was a way of keeping the memories alive. It had been 12 years since Esi, her husband Kofi and their eldest child, a daughter named Ama, had moved to Canada. Kobbey, born in the Shells Harbour hospital, had never been to his parents' homeland. Ama, three when they left, barely remembered it. Penny knew it was a wish of hers that they could travel to Ghana as a family before the children got too much older.

Penny admired how Esi straddled her two worlds. She wore a hand-knit Fair Isle sweater perfect for the North Atlantic winter along with a wax print cloth head wrap in bright shades of aquamarine, turquoise and navy blues that would have been, Penny guessed, a perfect fit in a market in the Ghanaian capital city, Accra. Earrings from the collection of jewellery she sold in a corner of her shop, made by a silversmith who lived in Montreal but was originally from Niger, dangled like mini daggers from her ears.

"When my grandmother would tell me stories, I would run to my cousins who lived on the other side of the compound and try to repeat them, but I could never remember how they ended. The kids would come into the house just as grandmother finished her tea to hear her tell the stories themselves," Esi said with a laugh. "My mother hated it because we were little clouds of dirt. But my grandmother loved telling her stories."

"You must miss it."

"Of course," Esi said. "But I'm happy here. We are happy and relieved here in a way we couldn't be back home. Kofi had gone as far as he could at the University of Ghana. There were some very old, fat men sitting in the way of any hope he had for advancing. That's just how the system works. And we knew that we would have to leave to build a life for ourselves. But sometimes," Esi let her words trail off.

"Sometimes what?"

Esi looked at her and shook her head.

"Sometimes I just want to feel it again. The heat, the sweat. Accra. I want to go to the market, see all the people moving here and there. Bite into a juicy mango straight off the tree. Put my hand into some fufu and groundnut soup, like my auntie used to make on Saturdays."

Esi looked deep into her cooling cup of tea, as if she could see the streets of her home city in the liquid. And maybe she could, Penny thought. Penny had left her hometown behind, pushing out thoughts of Shells Harbour when they nudged their way into her Toronto life. Esi had kept a piece of her heart in her home and it lived with her every day.

"We can't go back though, can we." Esi was making a statement, rather than asking a question. "I go visit, every few years, but the city is changing. So fast. No, we can't go back."

"I did," Penny said. "I came back."

But they both knew it wasn't the same. Esi shook her head.

"Maybe someday we can go visit. You and Sheila can come too," Esi said with a grin. Penny could tell that the reverie brought on by her memories had been pierced, and Esi's easy, but reserved, nature was back.

"If you went back to Ghana, you'd be spending most of your time catching up with friends and family," Penny said, and Esi nodded. "I've been the exact opposite. I think I've been hiding. When I knocked on Arlene's door and her son answered, it hit me how long I've been away.

Zach's almost a teenager now. And even though I'm back, I've still tried to keep away."

"I noticed you like to keep to yourself," Esi said. "I asked Sheila about it. She said you needed time."

"She might be right. But I don't think I have time anymore. I told Arlene I would figure out what happened to Vicki. I knew her a long time ago, but I need to talk to people who knew her now. People like you."

Esi exhaled out a long sigh but looked up from the mahogany-coloured wooden desk covered with papers and a laptop in the corner. She matched Penny's gaze.

"Then we're going to need another cup."

Esi's shop was smaller than Sheila's bookstore and didn't have a kitchen, so she simply poured water from the white electric kettle she kept on top of the shelf. The steam peeled from the water into the teapot and Esi placed the ceramic lid back on and waited. Penny hadn't known Esi for long, but she could tell that she was wrestling with something.

"My grandmother told me the story of a lady who ran my favourite candy shop. Some big man opened a rival shop for his mistress down the street, but everyone loved the other lady's store better. The big man told stories to her neighbours. He said she must have made a deal with the devil to be so successful in business or was a witch. Eventually people were scared enough that they stopped going."

Esi placed the refreshed mug of tea in front of Penny, who was absorbing the story. She knew herself how dangerous gossip could be, how it could drive people from their homes, their families and their community. Penny wondered how much Esi knew about Delphine, who shared the big man's habit of spreading lies to benefit herself.

She also wondered if town tales had somehow led Vicki Truitt to her death.

"I understand what you're saying, auntie. Around here, we all know what mean talk can do. Look at Mrs. Riggings. People wince when she talks, but we all lean in. Because as long as we know she's not talking about us, we want to hear what she says."

"I know," Esi said, but she offered no more. It might have just been that Esi wanted to register her disdain for gossip and make sure Penny knew she wasn't pleased to be telling stories about Vicki Truitt.

"Have you heard how her children are doing?" Esi changed the subject, without needing to mention Vicki's name.

"Arlene says Becky hasn't really figured out what's going on. Jared's just down in their basement, shooting pucks into a hockey net. Playing video games. Arlene said it's like he's just waiting for something to happen, someone to tell him what to do," Penny said. "Roger's back at the hospital already. Arlene said he brought the kids over to her house and dropped them off. They're out of school, but he went back to work."

Esi leaned back in her chair.

"I suppose everybody copes differently. Maybe he didn't want to let his patients down."

"Or he didn't want to lose out on the fees he'll collect for their visits," Penny said and Esi frowned. "I know. It's a horrible thing to say. But Arlene said Vicki had changed. It was all about money. And image. Arlene and Vicki were barely speaking before she died."

"People can be very strange about money, that's true," Esi said. "It was a problem for us, too."

"What do you mean?"

"On the Winter Carnival committee. Every cent had to be counted in Vicki's books. Which is fine, we are accountable to the public that donates to us, and money we get from the town council. But she was extreme." Esi paused to take a sip of her tea. Penny knew she was walking into territory that would make things uncomfortable for the woman who tried to avoid gossip.

"We needed to buy new chairs a few years ago. They were for the outdoor skating competition and the ice fishing derby, so they needed to be plastic. We like to support local businesses as much as we can, so one of our committee members got a quote from Sandmans."

Sandmans was a Shells Harbour institution, a locally owned

department store that the town supported with an almost aggressive pride. And Bill Pluckett, the third-generation owner, kept prices low enough that it was easy to choose to shop there.

"But Vicki said it wasn't good enough. She went up to the city, even out to the Valley, looking at other suppliers. The cost difference in buying the chairs from Sandmans would have been easily covered by the cost of getting anything out of town shipped down. And like I said, our policy is to buy local, where possible. It just didn't make sense that Vicki was being so fussy about it all," Esi said.

"What did the committee decide?"

"To buy from Sandmans, of course," Esi said. She glanced out of the front window of her travel agency. Penny followed her gaze. A man in a wool coat held the arm of an older woman bundled in a scarf and hat as they walked along the road sloping gently downhill toward the harbour. Two teenage boys ran past them, skidding on the snow and prompting the man to hold the woman a little tighter.

"Vicki's been chair for three years," Esi said. "And because we're accountable to the public and the town for the money we spend, we get our books audited after every carnival. I've been on the committee for six years now, and last year was the first time there was a problem."

"What kind of problem?"

"After the carnival, we take a few months off before we get together in late summer to plan for the following year. When we got together in August last year, Vicki said the audit wasn't done. That there were some problems with the numbers," Esi said. "But she said she was clearing it up with the auditors. And we shouldn't worry. It's no big deal, she said. The auditors told her things like this happen all the time."

"Things like what?"

"That's just it. She wouldn't be specific. No one else seemed too worried, so we let it go. But it stuck in my head," Esi said. "I run my business. I'm good with numbers. I helped Sheila sort out her books, you know," she laughed. "What a mess that was!"

Penny laughed and nodded.

"I remember, there were some very stressed-out messages left on my phone during that time."

"But we got it worked out, and I saved her some money to boot," Esi said. "I offered at the next meeting to help Vicki with anything she might need. With the audit, or with the books. Because, like I said, we never had a problem before. I thought maybe she was a little in over her head."

"And was she?"

"I think so. But I never actually found out. She wouldn't let me help her. She wouldn't let me see the books." Esi took a breath. "I told Lowell Cranson."

"The deputy mayor?"

"Yes. He's on the committee as the representative for the town. He told me not to worry about it. He said he would discuss it with Vicki. And I didn't hear anything else about it."

"When was this?"

"New Year's Eve, actually. Lowell was decorating the town hall for the levee the next day and I pulled him aside."

The New Year's Day Levee was a town tradition, a get together to celebrate the start of another year. It was the first time Penny had appeared in public since returning to Shells Harbour. She had been unnerved from the moment they entered town hall, even though the levee attracted the town's older residents and she had seen none of her friends.

"So, what do you think was going on?"

"Honestly? I don't know. There was something about it all that didn't make sense. She was so particular about money but seemed so lost at the same time."

"Maybe she wasn't lost," Penny said. "Maybe she knew what she was doing."

"What do you mean?"

"Maybe she controlled everything so tightly because she had a reason to keep her eyes on it. And maybe the deputy mayor wanted you to stay out of it," Penny said. She leaned forward as she spoke, her hands turning into tight fists under the edge of the desk in what she realized was another nervous habit.

Esi's mind was orderly, linear. Her straight-line thinking had helped the family make big decisions with logic and reason. Big decisions like moving not just to Canada, but to a small town where minds weren't exactly open to newcomers. Especially those who looked and sounded different than most of the people who move to the seaside town. Strawberry farmers had brought in migrant workers to pick berries during the peak weeks of the season, but they kept to themselves. There had been refugees resettled when the government sponsored people from countries in crisis, but over time, they filtered out of the rural town and into bigger cities. Most of the immigrants to Shells Harbour were white and European or American.

Esi had worked hard to find a place in Shells Harbour for her family. While Kofi drove to the city every day to teach at the university, Esi opened her business. She sat on the Winter Carnival board and learned all about hockey when Kobbey wanted to play like his friends. Ama was more reserved until the teenager found art that Esi displayed in her shop, bright watercolours that mashed up the cities of the world she dreamed of visiting with the rough coastal scenes of the Atlantic.

Esi and her family had settled. As Penny got to know them, she admired how they had made Shells Harbour home. More of a home than she ever had. Approaching the deputy mayor with her concerns over Vicki Truitt and the audit of the Winter Carnival's finances was a chance she would have debated fully before taking.

"I was hoping it was just a misunderstanding," Esi said. "I was hoping they would complete the audit and find nothing wrong. Maybe she'd made a math error or lost a few receipts."

"So, what happens now that she's gone?"

"I really don't know," Esi said. "Lowell wanted things to just go away, and maybe now they will."

Ten

The sun had fully risen, and roads were melting clear. There were two ways out of Shells Harbour and Penny picked the longer one, passing by Outcrop Road where the vehicle fire was that brought Paul and the fire department.

Around a bend in the road that followed the Atlantic coastline, Penny came to the entrance for the gravel pit where she and her friends had celebrated their high school graduation. It had been more than a decade, closer to a decade and a half. But for a moment, she thought of the cheap wine and beer that flowed that night. Her friends were close by and the town far enough away that no neighbour would call the police when they pumped music from a car stereo and lit a bonfire of damp spring firewood that coiled white smoke into the air. She slowed as she drove past the pit before finding a clear spot on the road to stop her Volkswagen.

Penny's stomach lurched as she opened her door. The fire trucks were parked in a very familiar place, more familiar than the gravel pit. She should have recognized the address when the dispatcher called it out on Paul's radio. She felt the heel of her boot skid along a patch of icy slush at the edge of the road and she clutched at her car to pull herself straight. So many corners of Shells Harbour held memories for Penny that followed her like a dull toothache to Toronto. But the Barkson house was one of the few places where she felt at ease.

Firefighters filled its snowy, tree-lined driveway. Alternating red and white lights rotated along the side of the house. Penny waited as a truck laden with cut logs swept along the curving road before she crossed over and followed the tracks of the firefighters into the driveway.

Penny saw Paul, again wearing the white deputy chief's helmet she had seen him in at the fire at Coleman's house. The one that reminded her of her grandfather, Harold Pintz. An icy wind swept around the open yard and Penny pulled her scarf up over her nose to protect her face from the frigid air and the smoky metallic tang of Albert Barkson's old, and now burned-out, pickup truck.

Albert and Mary Barkson lived in the house for most of their married lives. Albert had died more than a decade earlier and Mary was now in the Lazy Pines seniors' apartment complex in town. The decision to move her added to the conflict between Arlene and Vicki, their granddaughters.

The truck was a dark blue Chevrolet from the 1970s. It had been Albert's pride. He wasn't a mechanic, but Penny remembered afternoons when she and Arlene hopped off the school bus and walked up the driveway to the clang of Albert's wrench and his inevitable curse words when his repair didn't work. He knew enough about his truck to keep it on the road, but it surprised Penny that a decade after his death, no one had thought to get rid of it.

It was ruined now. Penny glanced around the house she hadn't seen in years. It made little sense. Nothing else about the property was touched. Albert's truck was old and had likely sat untouched for years. Vicki was dead, and Albert's truck catches on fire.

Someone has it out for the Barkson family, Penny thought, shaking her head in confusion.

She walked alongside the house and approached it how she did as a child. Not through the front door, but through the side door off the porch that entered the kitchen. She instinctively tried the door handle, but it was locked. Penny moved to the front of house, walking through the snow up a short knoll that gave the house its height to tower over the yard. She cupped her hands against a picture window to look into the living room. Her warm breath quickly fogged over the cool glass. She wiped it away and looked at the dark room inside.

A flutter of movement in the hallway beyond the living room caught her eye. She blinked. The house should have been empty.

"Whatcha doing up there?"

Jacob Bell called to Penny as she peered into the window. He was in the driveway below the hill and the crunch of his heavy fire boots on the snow hadn't registered for Penny, who was peering into the window to see more movement in the house.

She took a quick step backward and felt her ankle roll in a deep patch of snow. Her legs wobbled, and she tumbled into the cold snow, backside first. She cursed, and Jacob stepped ahead to help her.

"Did I scare you? I'm sorry." Jacob pulled off a black glove and extended his hand.

"No, it's not your fault," Penny said, putting her snowy, gloved hand into his bare one and apologizing. "I was just snooping. I saw the trucks on the road and I thought there might have been something going on at the house. I was going to see if Arlene was here. I was heading to Oaktown and knew the fire department had been called out here because Paul was in the bookstore when the alarm went."

She righted herself and stepped out of the patch of snow at the foot of the small hill. She knew she was talking too much and Jacob's friendly smirk showed her he did, too.

"It's okay, Peepee, you're not in trouble. We get a lot of lookie-loos on our calls. We're used to it. Just don't film me and put me on social media."

Penny laughed. "Not a chance." She brushed snow from her jeans, and Jacob slid his hand back inside his glove. "It's strange," Penny said. "I know the house is empty, but I swear I saw something moving inside."

Jacob looked at the quiet home. The lights from the fire trucks still cast a glow against the white siding and dark windows. "There was someone living there for a few months, I think. A renter. But as far as I know, it's been closed for a while now."

"That's what I thought. Maybe it was a trick of the light."

But Penny still felt uneasy as she followed Jacob along the tracks in the driveway flattened by the fire trucks. She turned her attention from the house to the burned remains of the Chevrolet.

"What happened to Albert's truck?"

"You remember that old beast? Remember how Arlene would drive it to school?" Jacob laughed.

"Oh yes, I do. There was that time we were in history class and she was late and she came rumbling into the parking lot. We all heard it. She couldn't sneak around with that truck," Penny said.

"Looks like someone tried to start it up. It's probably been sitting there half rotted out for years. Someone out on the road heard a boom and called it in."

"Who would have tried to drive it?"

Jacob shook his head and took off his red helmet. He ran his bare hand through hair damp from sweat despite the bitter day. His eyes narrowed at the corners. Penny thought he looked tired, but maybe that's how she looked, too. Neither of them were teenagers anymore, and they hadn't made it into their thirties unscathed.

"No idea. No trace of anyone when we got here," he said. "More bad news for Arlene. That woman has enough on her plate."

"You say someone tried to start the truck, and I'm certain I saw something moving around inside the house," Penny said, looking back over her shoulder at the quiet house. The darkened windows were like eyes watching the firefighters at work. "Did you call Arlene yet?"

"I think the chief did," Jacob said. "But let's face it, probably just some kids tried their luck with it."

"But you can't even see the truck or the house from the road," Penny said. "Someone was doing a lot more than trying their luck if they came up here to start it."

"Alright, so if someone was up here trying to start the truck, why would they run into the house? And anyway, I saw you try to open the door. It was locked, right?"

Penny nodded. "You're right. I'm probably imagining things. I'm a little worked up with everything going on, I guess." But Penny couldn't shake the feeling something hid behind the dirty white shingles and dark blue window frames.

"We're about done here. The guys will start packing up the hose soon. I'll make sure that Arlene has been told. Maybe she should look at putting in some security cameras. Or just finally getting rid of this place."

"She was trying, you know. She told me she wanted it to be Mary's decision, since it's still her house and all. Although it seems Vicki forgot that. She wanted the house sold and money in her pocket yesterday."

"Money?"

"Vicki tried to convince Arlene they could get a lot of money for this house, and the land with it. She told Arlene that their grandmother probably wasn't going to be around much longer. And since their mother is already dead and Albert and Mary had no other children, they could split the money."

"Arlene wouldn't care about that. She'd probably put it all in a fund for her kid," Jacob said. Another firefighter summoned for Jacob's attention through the radio that he had tucked into the front pocket of his bunker gear. Jacob clearly understood the words that sounded garbled to Penny.

"Copy that, let's roll out," he replied into the mic clipped to his open collar. "You're talking to Arlene? I'm glad to hear that. She probably needs a friend right now."

"She asked me to help find out what happened to Vicki. Since it seems the police aren't doing anything."

Jacob scoffed. "Tell me about it. I'm set up to investigate a fire, but a death is beyond my capacity. Try telling that to the Shells Harbour police. Detective Sutton wants me to figure it all out, and I don't want to let Vicki's family down."

"Maybe I can help. I've been talking to people who knew Vicki from the Winter Carnival committee. Maybe if we can find out a few leads to give to the cops, it will help me with Arlene and you with your fire investigation."

Jacob and Penny had moved further away from the house and

back toward the trucks. The firefighters were sitting inside the warm vehicles, looking at Captain Bell.

"I gotta get these guys back to the hall," he said. "Why don't you swing by later? I'll be there until about five."

Penny agreed. She walked back to her car, thinking about her drive to Oaktown, where she'd go to the women's store in the mall and look for a decent outfit for Vicki's memorial. She slipped back into her Volkswagen, turning the heat on high as she rubbed her hands together.

For a moment she paused and watched the large red trucks, their flashing lights turned off, pull away from the house. There was an allure to the idea of being a firefighter. It would be satisfying to help someone in their worst moments.

But then, that's what she was determined to do for her best friend. And if she was going to help Arlene find out the truth about what happened to her sister, Jacob, with his responsibility of investigating the fire, might be the best one to help her get it. As she slowly pulled back onto the deserted Outcrop Road, Penny glanced at the upper windows of the Barkson house, visible over the tops of the bare winter trees. She looked for a ripple in the closed curtains, a sign someone inside might be watching the trucks leave. But the house was as steady and calm as the glassy ocean on a hot summer morning.

Eleven

Penny glanced around Jacob's office as he took his laptop off his desk and set it on his chair. He had a cramped space above the fire hall's apparatus bay that held trucks and equipment. His office was made even more narrow by a line of filing cabinets stacked with boxes jutting into the space. The walls had thumbtacked maps of the Shells Harbour region, boiled down into house-by-house detail. Jacob looked at Penny as she surveyed the room. He ran a hand along his jaw like he was trying to massage out some invisible tension.

"I'm going to digitize all that," he said. "Someday."

Penny shrugged. She'd seen worse. "This is about the size of my first apartment in Toronto."

Jacob dropped his hand from his face and cleared some papers from a chair, gesturing for her to sit. On the space on his desk, Jacob spread the photos from Coleridge Coleman's half-burned mobile home. As Penny peered down, Jacob put his hand over the pictures.

"Listen, you and I both want to give some answers to Arlene. But I need to know you're not gonna go telling everyone what we might find out."

Penny smiled. "This is just like grade eleven physics all over again, isn't it?" Jacob twisted his head around to look at her, eyebrows raised.

"You were so paranoid that I'd tell Arlene about our laser light refraction project that you tried to ban me from going to her birthday sleepover."

Jacob turned to face her fully and laughed. "And I was right, wasn't

I? Her and Nick Parker showed up at the science fair with almost the exact same project."

"That wasn't my fault. You know Nick was spying on us after school. You caught him looking in the classroom door."

"I just really wanted that first prize. Fifty bucks. He didn't have to tell the principal I threatened to slash his tires. Like I would have."

Penny and Jacob laughed.

"I have proven that we can work together. And that I can keep a secret. Plus, the book publisher I worked for in Toronto had me reading all kinds of mysteries, so I know every plot twist out there. Can I see the pictures?"

He smiled and turned back to the pictures. He pointed to a black smear on a photo from the interior of the mobile home.

"See? See that?" He tapped at the picture that looked to Penny like someone had taken a smudge of charcoal and drawn it along a wall.

"What am I seeing?"

"That pattern of charring is enough to tell me this needs a proper investigation."

"Isn't that what you're doing?"

"Well, yes, but I'm not the police. Like I said over at the Barkson house, Detective Sutton wants me to do the work. I've been down this road before with him. Just send whatever you get, he tells me. And then he'll swoop in and make an arrest and half the time bungle it up enough that the case gets thrown out."

Jacob took a large sip of his coffee and peered down at the photos of the bedroom where the firefighters found Vicki.

"Whoever set this must have thought the fire would burn long enough to hide more evidence, even consume her body. But it takes longer than you might think to do that, and this person couldn't have known someone would be right behind them to call 9-1-1 so quickly." Jacob tapped at a spot on the picture. "That's where guys found her. Halfway under the bed on the right side, near the window."

"Near the window? Was she trying to get out?" Penny asked. The image of a desperate Vicki trying to find a way out of a room filled with toxic smoke swamped Penny's mind. She put her hand to her chest and tried to quash the thought.

The phone rang on Jacob's desk and he pushed aside a photograph of Coleman's cluttered yard to tap a button on the phone.

"Fire director's office," he said, keeping his eyes on the photographs, as if an answer would emerge from them.

"Jacob Bell?" A woman's voice came through the open speaker on the phone. "I'm Dr. Alash, with the medical examiner's office in the city. I was told by Detective Sutton to call you."

"He said you should call me?" Jacob looked at Penny and shook his head. "What can I help you with?"

"I have the information right here." Jacob tapped a pen against his thigh as the doctor shuffled papers on the other end. "Here we go. Vicki Truitt. She was found in a fire down your way?"

"Yes, that's right. She had no signs of life when the firefighters pulled her out."

"Well, that's no surprise. She was dead before the fire. There's no evidence of smoke in her lungs."

Penny absorbed Dr. Alash's words, but stayed quiet, knowing that Jacob was doing her a favour by allowing her to listen in on the call.

"So that means someone put her there?" Jacob asked.

"Or she was alive, and died there before the fire started," the doctor said. "I can't tell you which one. I can tell you she took a big blow to the back of her head."

Penny wrapped her hand around her mouth to keep her breath from escaping with a gasp. A vision of Vicki being attacked from behind flooded her mind. She caught Jacob's eye, and he glanced away. Penny knew her face showed every ounce of the dismay roiling her stomach.

"There would have been a fair amount of blood. And the wound was wide but narrow, which leads me to think it was likely made with a lot of concentrated force."

Jacob glanced down at the pictures of the bedroom and Penny followed. She saw no signs of crimson stains.

"There was quite a lot of congealing of the blood around the wound. It saturated her hair."

Penny thought of the long, blond hair draped between the firefighters who took her from Coleridge's home. Then, her mind floated to the night of Vicki's junior prom in high school. She had to be convinced to go. That was the year the rumours about her and Leonard Panzer, the owner of Panzer's Pizza, swept through town. Jacob asked his cousin Johnny to be Vicki's date. Like proud parents, Penny, Arlene and Jacob stood outside, snapping photos and waving as Johnny and Vicki pulled away from the sidewalk in Jacob's freshly washed Jeep. The late spring breeze scooped up Vicki's blond strands, and they floated out of the car window as the pair headed to the dance.

"She couldn't have died inside that trailer," Jacob said, more to himself than to the voice on the other end of the phone line.

"I'll send you a copy of my report. What's your email address?"

Jacob gave Dr. Alash the information and hung up. Penny pushed herself out of her chair and stood next to him at the desk, strewn with photos from what was now certainly a crime scene.

Jacob took plenty of pictures of the yard around Coleridge Coleman's home. Penny, who focused on photos of the charred bedroom where Vicki had been found, cast a glance at the ones Jacob eyed. Coleman's yard was a cluttered mess, with a broken television left to the elements, couches probably infested with rats, chairs discarded by the roadside and picked up by Coleridge. He was a chronic scavenger.

"It would be easy to hide something in that yard," she said. "Or the woods."

"Like a lot of blood."

"Have you talked to the owner of the mobile home?"

Jacob shook his head. "Can't find him. Coleman's known to go far and wide looking for things to add to his collection, but no one around town is sure where he's gone this time."

Penny knew Coleridge Coleman was a man at the edges of Shells Harbour, in his cluttered property off Hatchery Road. His closest neighbour was Mariner's Sawmill. He lived on the outskirts of town and its culture, community, and society.

"He came about 20 years ago. Which makes him fresh off the boat, by Shells Harbour standards," Jacob said. Penny nodded. Only people who could trace their roots back at least three generations were considered truly local. "He picked up work at the lumber yard there next to his trailer, but one day he took a chunk out of his thigh with a chainsaw. It never healed right and he couldn't work properly after that."

Penny winced at the thought. Coleman scraped by collecting discarded things to scrap for metal or other saleable parts. It would have been a hard life, and one that wouldn't have likely brought him into routine contact with Vicki Truitt, the doctor's wife, hockey mom and Winter Carnival board chair.

"I guess that leg injury rules out Coleridge as the person I saw on the trail right before I found the fire," Penny said.

"Oh yeah, he wouldn't be able to run a step."

"If he collected scrap, is there any reason to think he was going after Albert Barkson's truck? Arlene said he used to cut her grandfather's wood. He might have known it was there in the yard, abandoned."

Jacob ran his hand over his jaw again, rubbing his fingers into his cheek. He was silent for a minute.

"I don't know, Pen. Far as I know, Coleridge is not one to look for trouble. He just keeps to himself. But with his trailer burned, he might be desperate."

"It just seems odd, doesn't it? Two things have now happened to Arlene's family. And there could be a connection with Coleridge Coleman between both fires."

"Maybe there's your plot twist," Jacob said. His phone buzzed with an incoming text message. He read the screen and nodded.

"I asked my buddy who works at Mariner's to keep an eye on the road and let me know if Coleman or anyone else came to the house. And his truck just turned into the yard."

Twelve

Coleridge Coleman stared at the half-burned shell of his mobile home. He said nothing. Penny and Jacob had pulled into the driveway but, for a long minute, they left the man alone with the fire's aftermath.

He looked battered by life. His checkered jacket hung off his shoulders, with the lining frayed and falling loose out of the hem. His baggy jeans, oversized for his gaunt body, were half tucked into work boots that had their tongues hanging loose like tired dogs.

Finally, Jacob took the lead and swung himself out of the driver's seat of his pickup. On the way over, he'd told Penny about a few fire calls he'd had to Coleridge's property, when someone driving by would see a plume of smoke, and it would be Coleridge burning piles of trash. He'd sour when the fire department inevitably put the bonfire out, so Jacob had warned Penny that Coleridge Coleman might not be happy to see him.

"Mr. Coleman," Jacob said. "We need to talk."

Coleridge still didn't acknowledge Penny and Jacob's presence, although he had glanced at the truck as they came into the yard. Instead, he stomped into the trailer, making footprints in the snow that had fallen on the charred home.

"Be careful, Coleridge," Jacob said, following behind as the man picked his way into what had been the kitchen. Penny edged into the home too and stifled a sigh at the sight of the wreckage. The fire might have started in the bedroom, but the stains of smoke had spread through the mobile home.

The narrow hallway, barely three feet wide, would have been tough for firefighters and the bulky gear Penny saw them wear. Hose water soaked the carpet, which squished underneath their boots. As she watched Coleridge and Jacob step along the hall to the bedroom, Penny imagined the challenge of bringing Vicki Truitt's body along that narrow route. Not just for the firefighters, but for her killer, as well, if they attacked Vicki outside of the home.

"Do you have insurance?" Jacob spoke first.

Coleridge grunted in response.

The parts of the trailer that saw less damage showed a home that was austere and tidy, unlike the cluttered yard. There was a small television in the wood-panelled living room and a plastic outdoor table and chairs for a dining set. There were no pictures on the wall, just a poster of a race car and an ornately framed photograph of a soaring eagle.

"I got it from here, Bell," he said. "Don't got no insurance and don't need no help."

But Penny knew it wouldn't be that simple. Coleridge was gone when someone set his trailer on fire with Vicki Truitt's body inside. And he was still gone for days afterward until he reappeared just as suddenly as he'd left. Penny figured he was the type to want time and space to himself, to keep the prying eyes of Shells Harbour out of his business. She could relate to that. But the eyes were now hers and Jacob's.

"It's not just about what help I can give you," Jacob said. "You know I'm the fire director for Shells Harbour. Someone committed a crime here and I have to find out what happened and why."

"I don't know nothing about a crime." Coleridge folded his thin arms across the chest of his woodsman's jacket, puffing up his stature.

"Coleridge, did you know Vicki Truitt?" Penny asked him. She realized that he wouldn't know who she was, but she hoped that wouldn't stop him from answering her.

"She the one that died in here?"

"Yes. She was the wife of Dr. Truitt, over at the hospital. They had two little ones," Jacob said. Penny wondered how, if Coleridge had been out of town, he knew about the death. She watched him for any reaction to what Jacob had said.

But Coleridge simply shook his head and looked around the charred bedroom. Every piece of furniture in the small room had been blackened.

"Do you know what she was doing here?" Penny asked.

"I got no clue. Wouldn't know who she was if my life depended on it," he said. "And who the frig are you to be asking me these questions? I don't owe you no explanations."

Penny knew Coleridge was right, but she was stuck for an answer to give him. She thought about what Dr. Alash said, that Vicki's head wound would have elicited a great pool of blood. She looked around the room but if there was blood, it was lost in the sooty, soaking mess.

"You owe me an explanation, though," Jacob said. "I'm investigating this fire just like I do every other time we have to come out here."

Penny knew Jacob's reference to "we" was about the fire department, but she didn't feel a need to make that clear to Coleman. He could think she was a member of the department if it kept him talking.

"This where you found her?"

Jacob nodded. "Two of my men pulled her out. Tried to do resuscitation, but it was clear. She was gone before we got to her."

Coleridge Coleman showed little surprise at this information. Apart from rubbing his dirty fingernails through shaggy beard, he showed little emotion at all.

Until something cracked open inside him. The sight of the charred bedroom, the frozen pools of water, maybe even, Penny thought, the knowledge that a life had been lost there.

"Gawdammit," he hollered with a force that sent Jacob taking a protective step backward further from Coleman and into Penny, who stumbled and tripped over a debris pile. Jacob turned to help her up while Coleman flung open the accordion doors of his narrow closet and began pulling out the few items of clothing he had in there, and tossing them on a corner of the sooty, soggy bed.

"What are you doing?"

"Gettin' what I can get," Coleridge growled.

"Do you want me to call the Red Cross? They can set you up in temporary housing," Jacob said.

"Nope, no way. I shoulda never left this place. This is my property. I ain't leaving again, no sir."

"You can't stay here."

"I ain't goin' nowhere. Got a stove out in the back building. That'll be fine till I can figure out what to do."

"It's going down to minus 10 tonight," Jacob said. "Colder with the wind chill."

Coleridge tugged open the drawers on a blond wood dresser and began grabbing pairs of wool socks that had somehow been spared damage.

"I don't care. I ain't leaving. I don't know what happened here, but I ain't gonna let nothing happen again," he said. "Now, I gotta get these here clothes out and over to the building. I think I ain't got nothing else to say."

Jacob nodded, and Penny sensed Coleridge wasn't the type to have his mind changed.

"Alright," Jacob said, reaching into the side pocket of his blue uniform cargo pants. He pulled out a business card and pressed it into Coleridge's calloused hands. "My cell number's on there. Call me anytime. Don't freeze out there."

Outside the home, Penny dusted soot off her jeans and eyed Coleridge as he carted clothes stuffed in a battered hockey bag from his house to the back shed. She looked at Jacob.

"You just gave your phone number to a man who might be a victim of this fire or might be something else entirely."

Jacob looked at her. "I'm aware of that," he began walking across the yard with its layer of crunchy snowfall. He clicked the lock to open the doors to his truck. "But did he seem like someone who had any idea what had happened in his home?"

"No, unless he's Meryl Streep in a beard, he seemed genuinely shocked."

Jacob and Penny lifted themselves into his still-warm pickup truck.

"Besides," Jacob said, taking one last look in the rear-view mirror as he pulled away from the charred home, "why would he come back? If he had killed Vicki, either in that bedroom or somewhere else, and dragged her body into the trailer, set it on fire and fled, why come back?"

"Unfinished business?" Penny said. "He said he wouldn't let anything else happen here. Doesn't that sound like he might anticipate more trouble?"

"I think you're reading a lot into someone who's pretty upset right now," Jacob said. "We should be thinking more about Vicki Truitt than Coleridge Coleman. People in town know that he will go away for several days at a time. Vicki's killer might have just needed a quiet place."

Jacob steered his pickup along Hatchery Road, back toward Shells Harbour. Coleridge's home was just a few minutes from the town but it felt isolated, remote. Penny watched the churning Atlantic lap winter waves at the short cliffs that edged the road.

"You guys get a lot of calls out here? This road was always bad in the winter, with the storm water spraying."

"All year long. In winter it's the ice, in summer it's the tourists trying to get the perfect shot, and not paying attention to what's coming the other way."

"You must see some awful things."

"Sometimes."

Penny held the silence for a moment. Classic rock played lightly from Jacob's stereo. She imagined the fear someone would feel, careening off the road and wondering if help was going to come. Vicki might never have had the chance to even be afraid.

"How long have you been the town fire director?"

"About five years," Jacob said. "I was working at Prime Ocean after graduating, but I always wanted to make a career in the fire service. I trained online and drove up to the city for classes."

"Did you ever think about leaving? Taking a job in one of the career departments where you can get paid?"

"Thought about it. Then Chris came along. His mother has never wanted to leave Shells Harbour, even when we were together. After we split up, I knew I didn't want to be a weekend and holidays dad. So here I stay. I got the director's job when it came up and that keeps me close when calls come in."

"But when you're on a fire call, you don't get paid, right?"

Jacob shook his head. "We're an all-volunteer department. I get paid for what I do with the town, but not with the department. Although, there are times like now, when the two sides come together."

"I understand the part of it that's your job, but why do you give up so much of yourself for this town, for all the time you're not getting paid for?"

"This town is us, Penny. These people are us. We do it for each other. Even when I was still working at the fish plant, I was a volunteer firefighter. Cause someone needs to be there on our worst days."

Penny let the silence filter through the truck.

"Nobody was there for Vicki on her worst day. I wasn't fast enough."

"No, we weren't," Jacob said. "But we can be there for her now."

"And for Arlene," Penny said, as Jacob pulled his truck into his parking spot at the fire station. "Thank you for taking me to see Coleridge. I know you don't have to include me in this, but I'm glad you are." She held his blue eyes for a moment and saw distance in them, as if he was thinking about something much farther away than the trailer. Her gloved hand reached for the door handle.

The heat in the truck had made her eyes heavy-lidded, and she stretched out for the fresh, cold air of Shells Harbour.

"I'll see you at Vicki's memorial."

Thirteen

Sheila crouched behind Brittle Pages' wooden sales counter, sorting through the latest box of books. Penny smiled at the sight of her aunt in the pose that she remembered well from her teenage years, when she'd come to the bookstore after school to tend customers while Sheila ran errands. Her aunt was always buried under a pile of books, with wispy hair flipping loose from a braid. The only thing different about this scene now was a greyer braid and deeper smile lines around her aunt's eyes.

But then, Penny thought, she had changed, too. A few grey hairs of her own met her in her early 30s, and her fashion sense matured from baggy jeans with holes in the knees and ratty t-shirts to warm sweaters and winter boots. Penny was, she liked to think, more responsible with her health than she had been in high school, when she and Arlene lived on a diet of pizza they would get from Vicki behind the counter at Panzer's. Sheila glanced up at the door chime.

"You're back," she said. "Did you find what you needed at the mall?"

Penny had almost forgotten about the outfit of black slacks and a navy knit pullover that she'd found in the Oaktown Mall.

"I did. I believe I will blend in nicely with my bland option."

Sheila offered Penny an eye roll. "It's a funeral, girl, not a party in your gravel pit."

Penny laughed. Sheila never offended her when she dressed her down affectionately, like the teenager Penny once was. No matter how many grey hairs started showing up in her brown ponytail, Sheila would always see her as a girl.

Sheila glanced over Penny's shoulder. "We're getting a customer."

Penny turned to follow her aunt's gaze. Erin Riggings pressed her cupped hands against the Brittle Pages picture window, peering into the shop around the foggy glaze her breath created on the glass.

She pulled back quickly when she saw the two women inside, looking back at her. Sheila offered a gentle wave, calling her in.

Erin was in a bright, flowered coat and had wrapped a pink scarf around her neck as a ward against the cold. Her ears were scarlet under the soft curls of her grey hair and she reached in a pocket of her jacket for a tissue to wipe her nose.

"Are you sick, Erin?" Sheila asked by way of a greeting. But the woman shook her head.

"No, this bloody winter. Up and down, up and down. I wish we could stick to a temperature and that's it until spring. I used to think all this global warming stuff was nonsense, but winters weren't like this when I was a kid."

"It's definitely not nonsense," Penny said, stifling her own eye roll as she remembered to be polite to Sheila's customers.

"I said I *used* to think that," Erin replied with an edge in her voice that made Penny wonder if she was there to shop at all.

"We've got a few books on that, if you want to inform yourself," Sheila said. "I can recommend several."

"Oh, enough of that," Erin said. She turned to face Penny. "I have a bone to pick with you, little missy."

"Me?" Penny was mystified. She barely knew Erin Riggings and the older woman was scolding her like she was a student about to get detention.

"Yes, you. You had me swanning around town here, trying to find out everything about Vicki Truitt's death when you knew her just as good as anyone. You were her sister's best friend. Tight as sardines in a can, I hear."

Penny felt heat rise to her face, but she wasn't sure what she was being accused of. To Erin, it seemed her crime was simply having a friend many years earlier.

"Yes, Arlene and I were in school together," Penny said. "I'm sorry to be rude, but what's that got to do with you, Mrs. Riggings?"

"Well, it's got everything to do with me," she said, blowing her leaky nose into the tattered tissue that she stuffed back in a pocket. "I need to know everything about Vicki. She was clearly leading some kind of double life."

"What on earth are you talking about, Erin?" Sheila said.

"You don't just go and turn up dead around here," Erin said. "You and I both know she must have had something going on. I'm betting this was —" Erin looked around the store before continuing. "Foul play."

Penny exchanged a look with Sheila. She knew that Jacob would have kept quiet the medical examiner's report confirming that Vicki had been dead before the fire. And she wasn't about to confirm Erin Riggings' suspicion.

But then, she remembered her conversation with Esi. About the odd financial dealings that seemed to be happening at the committee. Penny had a hard time believing Vicki's killing stemmed from a little community party, but she knew small towns could turn minor disputes into epic battles.

"Why didn't you tell us earlier you were on the Winter Carnival board with Vicki?" Penny asked Erin.

"Well, it just didn't seem right, at the time. To make it all about me. When poor Vicki wasn't even cold," Erin said. She shook her head with contrition that seemed staged for Penny and Sheila's benefit. Her curls quivered and, as if sensing they were now out of place, Erin reached a wrinkled hand up and patted her coiffure with manicured fingers.

Penny caught sight of her aunt, who was trying to stifle a smile. Sheila and Erin, Penny thought, must be similar in age, but were wholly different in character and appearance.

"Why would it be all about you, Mrs. Riggings?" Penny asked.

"Oh dear, please call me Erin. Well, you see, with Vicki gone, I'm now chair of the committee." Erin straightened her shoulders and lifted her chin. "It's a terrible shame it happened like this, although frankly, the committee needed a change."

Penny and Sheila exchanged quick glances, which Erin caught.

"Oh stop that. Of course I had nothing to do with her death," she said. "Honestly, we were probably going to vote her out after this year's carnival, anyway. Really, I hate speaking ill of the dead like this, but it's the truth."

"Who's we?" Penny asked.

"We — the committee, of course. I think even Esi was on board. She was the one who was raising a fuss anyway, going to the deputy mayor and all."

Sheila looked at Penny. "Did you know that?"

"Yes, did you?"

"I had an idea something was weighing very heavily on Esi these last few months. How did you know, Erin?"

"She had to tell us. I'm on the sub-committee for finance, anyway. If there was a problem with the books, I would have found out."

"The committee has sub-committees?"

"Oh yes, we have to plan everything out perfectly. There's a committee for the hockey game between the police and the fire department. There's one for the snow carving contest, one for the ice fishing derby. Trust me, if we don't have everything done just right, we hear about it. All year long."

Penny could hear the strain in Erin's voice. She thought again about how reluctant Esi was to talk about the Winter Carnival committee. It seemed like organizing a fun community event was really a heavy burden.

"If it's that much pressure, why would you want to be the chair?" Sheila asked. Penny could tell her question came from a place of honest curiosity. Erin lifted her nose an inch and attempted to look down at Sheila, even though Erin was a good half-foot shorter.

"Because I thought I could do it better. I'm certain of it. Vicki became chair after her husband pushed her on us," Erin said, lowering her voice, as if they were in a crowded place, rather than the quiet bookstore.

"Why?" Penny asked.

"He said, not in so many words but the message was clear, that he could see to it that the hospital's charity board pulled its funding of the carnival. Next to the town council, it's the biggest donor. The carnival wouldn't be even half of what it is now."

"And that would be a bad thing?" Penny said.

"Of course it would. Have you looked outside the bookstore lately? You and Sheila may not care that you sell just a few birthday cards and cookbooks every now and then until the spring melt, but winter hits most of the businesses in this town. Hard," Erin said. She gestured toward the quiet folk art and curios shop across Barque Lane. "When was the last time you saw someone leave Merrill's with so much as a shopping bag? The Lighthouse Inn closed the winter half of the B&B a month early — before Christmas this season. That's unheard of. No, the Winter Carnival, for some people in this town, feeds their families for a month with the tourists that come in. If anything, we need to make it bigger."

Penny listened to Erin's speech with an astonishment she tried to hide behind a neutral expression. She knew her aunt's shop was more of a labour of love, earning enough to pay the bills on the building, which she had owned mortgage-free since before Penny had left for university. Sheila inherited the house they shared. Penny chided herself quietly for not seeing beyond their privilege. Of course, the town's artisans, the ones who kept Shells Harbour on the map as one of the country's busiest summer tourist destinations, needed to have some income during the long winter months.

"Why was Roger Truitt so keen to have Vicki chair the committee?" Sheila asked.

"Same reason he wanted her volunteering at the hospital fundraisers, managing the boys' hockey team," Erin said.

"To keep her busy?" Penny said. Erin shrugged, glancing with a look that tried hard to be nonchalant at a stack of books on the counter. Penny pressed her further. "And why would he want to do that?"

"Why would a man want to keep his wife occupied? Distracted? That's not a question I can answer."

"Who could, Erin?" Sheila questioned. The woman hesitated. She brought a hand to her mouth and rubbed a smooth ruby stone embedded in a gold ring back and forth against her upper lip. It was probably an unconscious gesture, but to Penny, it showed that even this gossip might have felt like a step too far.

"There are four women on the committee. Well, there were. Now there are three. And I'm happily married. I'm not saying anything else." Erin held up her hands in a gesture of innocence, or surrender. "Now that I know you're close with Arlene, I want you to tell her I'm not happy about Vicki's death. This isn't how I wanted to take over the committee. It's a terrible tragedy and those two little darlings have lost their mother. I will do my duty for our community though, but I tell you, I'm not happy about it."

Erin pulled her purse strap tighter over her shoulder and turned on her heel, jangling the bell on the door as she tugged it open.

"She's right, of course, Pen," Sheila said. "Nothing else matters but those children."

"I know what you mean, but the kids are going to grow up hearing all kinds of talk and wondering where the truth is," Penny said. "Erin was right. Vicki's death wasn't an accident. Someone killed her."

"Oh, I can't believe this. There hasn't been a murder in Shells Harbour since — well, I have no idea when."

"Those kids, and Arlene and this whole town are going to wonder who did it. And why," Penny said. "Is that paper from yesterday still back there? With the committee list?"

Sheila glanced down at the counter and fished through a pile of books until she found the newspaper. She flipped it open on the empty counter and Penny peered at it from the opposite side.

"Here it is. Let's see. Vicki, Erin, here's Esi of course." Penny nodded.

"And Tammy Johnson," Sheila said, looking up from the paper. "You can talk to Paul about her."

"And Tammy Johnson," Sheila said, looking up from the paper. "You can talk to Paul about her."

Fourteen

The morning of Vicki Truitt's memorial came with another snowfall warning from the weather agency. The radio station in Oaktown had the storm starting late afternoon, just when the gathering was due to take place.

The forecast came in the mid-morning news bulletin that interrupted the station's usual stream of seventies rock. Penny pulled her car into a visitor's parking spot at the back of the Shells Harbour fire station as the news reader made quick mention of a fatal fire and ongoing investigation before an April Wine song played. Jacob's truck wasn't in the yard. But Paul's pickup was in the designated deputy chief's spot, so she knew he would be there.

When Penny was younger, she would wander into the fire hall after school, sometimes with Jacob and Arlene behind her, where they'd find her grandfather, Harold, working on a truck or grunting into a pile of paperwork. He'd let them into the firefighter's lounge with its cable television and snack machines they fed with their spare quarters.

It was different now. Newer trucks and gear. A television screen in the apparatus bay displayed a blinking digital record of recent alerts. Still, when she entered the hallway, the smell was the same: diesel-fuelled engines and smoky fire gear steeped in blazes long extinguished.

Deputy Chief Haines found Penny gazing through the window of a locked internal door at the fire trucks. Shells Harbour had five now, including a more modern version of the ladder truck Penny had loved as a child. Harold would hoist her on the back of the cab and show her the elaborate mechanical controls that were just shiny knobs and levers to her then. Penny saw a speedboat enhanced with lights and rescue gear that looked like it belonged to the coastguard or police. The department had made plenty of changes since she was a girl.

"It's in your blood," Paul said as he opened the internal door. "Fire-fighting. Are you here for a membership application?"

Penny turned back as she stepped through the door in front of his outstretched arm. She expected to see laughter in his eyes. But the deputy chief was clearly serious.

"I couldn't do what you do. What Jacob and the guys did the other day. Run into a burning building. Bringing someone out like that. Trying to help them and you can't," Penny shook her head, rambling. She loved the fire department for the memory of her grandfather, but the idea of being part of it herself fit her like a shoe a size too big. Awkward and off balance.

"We don't run into burning buildings. We walk with purpose," Paul said and offered her a smile that touched the corners of his eyes. "And you would be surprised what you are capable of. With the right train-ing. And the right people standing with you."

"The right people," Penny repeated. "That's what I came to talk to you about, one of your people. Can we speak somewhere?"

Paul swiped an electronic keycard and led Penny out to the floor of the wide bay that held the fire trucks, gleaming engines with sharp red angles, piles of beige, yellow and orange hoses, silver polished knobs and levers. Penny glanced at the large vehicles and for a moment thought of racing to the hall, throwing on the weighty gear and climbing into one of them to play a minor role in alleviating the agony of someone's terrible day. Paul glanced back at Penny as he led her past the trucks.

"Nice, aren't they? We may not be a big town, but we have a lot of pride in this department."

Paul led Penny through the apparatus bay floor and into a small office near the back of the large room. A bank of black radios was on a desk in front of them. Maps of the area and bookshelves filled with firefighting manuals and phone directories climbed the walls. He motioned to a black office style chair and Penny sat down.

"I'm starting to think there was something strange going on with the Winter Carnival committee," she said. "It seems there were moves to get Vicki Truitt out of the chairmanship role."

"Where did you hear that?"

"Erin Riggings. Not the most reliable source, I know, but I'm inclined to believe her. She seems really anxious about this whole thing. And if you can believe it, she clammed right up when Sheila and I pressed her on it. Would only hint about something to do with Roger wanting Vicki to be chair to keep her busy."

"Why would he want to do that?"

"Well, I guess that's why I'm here. Erin made a point of noting that there were four women on the committee. Herself, Vicki, Esi Gyan."

"And Tammy Johnson," Paul said.

"Right," Penny said, treading carefully. If there was one thing she remembered about her grandfather, it was the loyalty among firefighters. They supported each other and kept personal issues within the department. More than once, a firefighter having problems in his home life would take up residence in Harold and Ivy Pintz's spare bedroom as he figured out where to go after his wife kicked him out, or he tried to sober up from a few drinks too many.

"Tammy's a good firefighter. A good person," Paul said, unprompted. "I can't imagine she's involved. Is Erin trying to say she's mixed up in this? Something to do with Roger?"

"I don't know, honestly. I don't know how this all comes together," Penny said. "Esi was concerned enough to talk to the deputy mayor about some of the committee's financial problems. Although she didn't get very far with him."

As Penny and Paul delved further into the few details they knew about the case, the radios in the communications room came to life, sending Paul to his feet. It was a medical call, for an elderly woman struggling to breathe. Penny suspected those alarms were more common in Shells Harbour now, as residents grew older and younger ones were more likely to leave than stay.

With Paul in the passenger seat, a truck peeled out of the hall, lights and sirens lighting up the quiet morning. Penny waited in the communications room as a few more firefighters pulled into the hall and stood by to see if they were needed. She recognized some of the crew who were at the fire at Coleman's mobile home, and the burning truck at the Barkson house.

Penny watched an older man slide into the chair in the communications room that Paul had left unoccupied, barely giving her a glance as he focused on the bank of radios in front of him. It was only as he established a link between the dispatcher and the firefighters arriving on the scene that the man turned to Penny and introduced himself as Mason Arthur. Penny explained that she had been visiting the deputy chief when the call came in.

"Pintz, you said? You related to old man Harold?"

Penny nodded. "He was my grandfather. He'd bring me here all the time."

Mason spoke into his radio to confer with the crew who arrived at the senior's home but kept his eyes on Penny.

"I remember you now. You and Jacob and some of those other rugrats were over here a lot back then," Mason said. "Yep, I fought many a fire with your old grandpa."

Tammy Johnson arrived, and like the other firefighters, she headed to the communications room to sign the logbook that kept track of the crew who responded to the emergency call. Penny recognized her from the photo in the newspaper of the Winter Carnival committee.

"Hi," Penny said. "You're Tammy, right?"

Tammy looked at Penny and raised her eyebrows.

"I am," she said, with cautious curiosity. Mason took care of the introductions.

"Penny here is the old chief's granddaughter, Chief Pintz. Boy, he was a good chief. Always fighting with the town to get us something extra, some new gear or do-dads. We all thought he was a little nuts, but then we'd get whatever thing chief wanted and we'd all have to admit the old man was right. He was always looking out for us."

"It's good to meet you. Your grandfather's a legend round here," Tammy said. "You here to get an application? We need more women in the department." Penny was taken aback not only by another query about her interest in membership, but by Tammy's easy warmth.

She wasn't prepared to like the woman who might somehow be linked to Vicki's death.

"Couldn't agree more," Jacob Bell said, joining the growing group in the communications room. "The more diverse we are as a department, the better we reflect our community."

"Too bad we know yours isn't the unanimous opinion," Tammy said, in a way that made it clear she and Jacob had talked about it before.

"Really?" Penny asked. "There are people who still think women shouldn't be in the fire department."

Mason Arthur nodded. "Oh yes, I hear it around town. I guess some of the old timers think cause I'm over the hill myself I think the same way. They start going on about how if you can't hump a hose up ten flights of stairs, you got no business being a fireman. Forgetting the fact that even in their prime, half of those buggers were too out of shape to make it half that far."

"Stuck in their Shells Harbour ways," Tammy nodded.

"Sad part is, some of those voices come from places where you least expect," Mason said. "My wife tells me she hears women in the ladies' auxiliary complaining about female firefighters more than anyone else. Worried about their husbands in close quarters with other women."

Tammy crossed her arms in front of her chest and nodded in a way that showed she'd heard it before. A few strands of her blond hair that had escaped from her ponytail wavered.

"There are some real gossips out there. I always wonder if they called 9-1-1 when they set their kitchen on fire and I show up to put it out, would they turn me away and ask for a man?"

The unexpected turn in the conversation made Penny wonder. There was no bigger gossip in town than Erin Riggings, and if it was fashionable in some circles to complain about women in the fire department, Penny could see her feeding into the talk.

I don't know if Erin is capable of that, Penny thought. Would she really drop hints about a female member of the fire department to make it look like she was involved with a married man?

Though Penny grew up in Shells Harbour and knew what the small-town grist mill was like, she felt the need to question Tammy a bit more. Jacob had settled into a chair next to Mason and was tapping into the desktop computer, so Penny turned to Tammy.

"Would you mind showing me around a bit? I'd like to see how much the department has changed since I came here as a kid."

"And get her an application form while you're at it," Mason said with a teasing smile.

Fifteen

Penny followed Tammy out of the communications room. Penny pegged Tammy as in her early 40s, with an easy confidence around the fire equipment that made Penny think anyone should be happy to have her show up to put out their kitchen fire. As Tammy showed Penny the bulky gear she wore on calls, Penny saw an opening.

"Is it tough? Being a woman and a firefighter?"

"I'd be lying if I said I had no grief," Tammy responded. "You learn pretty quick who's got your back and who's waiting to see you fall."

"You mean within the community? Or the department?"

"To be honest, both. If you're thinking about joining, that would be great, but you gotta grow a bit of a thick skin to it all. Most people don't care. When you show up to pull someone out of a ditch or put out the trees that caught on fire when they were burning garbage they shouldn't have been, they don't see your gender. They see the flashing lights and that's about it."

"It must get frustrating, though. Do you talk to people about it?"

"Sometimes. Some of it you keep inside. I talk to the deputy chief. Mason's pretty understanding, too. My husband works away half the time on a freighter and when he's home we have his kids at our house, so he likes that I have the department to keep me occupied when he's not around. He says otherwise I'd be pining away for him," Tammy said with a quick laugh. "Course we both know I'd find something, but for the grief you get, it's worth it."

"That can't be easy, him being away that much. I'm surprised he doesn't worry about you around the guys here," Penny said. She cringed to herself about saying that to a woman she'd just met. Finding out what happened to Vicki was proving to Penny how awkward it was to ask questions, and pry into lives of people she'd just met.

"He trusts me. I've never given him a reason not to," Tammy replied. She glanced at Penny with a raised eyebrow. "Kind of strange that you're worried about my husband. You got a fella you think might not like you joining the department?"

"No, not at all actually," Penny thought, her mind flicking for a moment to her old boyfriend, Callum, whose opinion mattered far too much for too long. "I'm just getting used to how the local gossip mill works, and I was wondering if people talked about you being one of just a few women among all these guys. And maybe tried to make trouble in your marriage."

"Well, I suppose that could happen, but like I said, I haven't given my husband a reason to worry about the fellas in the department."

"What about outside the department?"

Tammy's eyebrows shot up. "Are you getting at something? We just met, so you don't know me, but I don't mince words and I don't like what you're implying."

Penny was coming to see there was an art to investigating crime in her small town, and it's one that she would have to work on if she was going to get answers for Arlene.

"I'm sorry, I didn't mean to upset you," Penny paused and decided to take a chance. She glanced around and realized the firefighters who had been lingering in the hall after the medical emergency call had dispersed, retreating to their regular lives. "Arlene Tanner is a good friend of mine. My best friend," Penny said. The words were odd to say as a grown woman, especially one who had stretched out more than a decade of almost no contact until just days earlier. Tammy nodded.

"It wasn't just that I called in the fire where you guys found Vicki. When I realized who was in there, I promised Arlene I would help her. And what she needed help with was finding out what happened."

"Vicki's death wasn't natural, was it?"

Penny didn't respond. She looked down at the dusty cement floor of the bay for a moment before raising her eyes and setting her lips into a thin grimace.

"It's fine, half the town probably knows, and the other half will find out tomorrow," Tammy said with a dry smile. "So where do I come in?"

"The Winter Carnival committee."

"Ah yes. The other thing that sucks up my time. From October to March, it's my life. We're having an emergency meeting tonight to figure out what we need to do and how to honour Vicki. So you're wondering if someone on the committee might have killed her?"

Tammy's frankness left Penny stuck for a response. The woman offered her another thin smile. "I told you I don't mince my words."

"I see that. Honestly, I don't know. Someone on the committee suggested I talk to you about all of this. And about Vicki's husband."

"Dr. Truitt?" Tammy paused. "Ah. I see. That's why you were asking about my husband. Someone's saying I've got something going on with Roger Truitt. Wait, no. Not someone. I don't even need to guess. Erin Riggings."

Penny stayed silent, figuring that her lack of a denial was confirmation enough. She wondered what pitting these two strong women against each other would bring, both for her investigation and for the Winter Carnival committee.

"Roger and I curled together last winter, and I know tongues wagged when he dropped me off at home a few times from the rink. Erin has a mean streak and she's had her eye on committee chair for a while. She's had it out for Roger because of how he pushed Vicki on us. And she probably sees me as a threat."

"She said she's already chair."

Tammy's chuckle seemed to come from somewhere deep in her belly. "It doesn't work like that," she said. "We have to vote in the chair. It's in our bylaws, if Erin would bother to read them."

"Is Erin right to see you as a threat?"

Tammy exhaled and bent over to pick up a black glove that had fallen out of someone's gear. She looked at the names on top of the compartments where rows of helmets, boots, jackets, and pants hung.

"There's a part of me that thinks I'd do a good enough job, yeah. But a bigger part of me was thinking I'd give up the committee after this year. Too much drama. And now too many questions," Tammy paused, glancing around at the empty hall to make sure there were no hidden ears listening. "Do you know about the money stuff?"

"I know questions have been raised about the spending, and the committee's auditors brought up problems with the books."

Tammy nodded. "It's not good. I'm on the financial review committee and the auditor sent us a letter outlining a gap of about ten grand in the budget. That was just for last year. They said based on that, they need to do a forensic examination of past years. This is the first year we've hired an outside auditor, and it's only because of these new regulations from the province after the debacle at the Farm Fair in the Valley a few years ago."

"What happened there? I must admit, I didn't pay much attention to Nova Scotia news when I was living in Toronto."

"The fair rigged supply deals, inflating the prices and offering contracts to vendors who were sliding back the difference to the committee and keeping a cut for themselves. It all came to light when the bleachers collapsed. A bunch of people got hurt and when they investigated, it turned out that the bleachers were about 60 years old and had been in some high school storage shed for about a decade, rotting away. The vendor had billed the town for brand new bleachers and just slapped paint over the old ones."

Penny shook her head. "Is that what's going on here?"

"I think it's possible. Vicki had me running all over to look at suppliers for chairs when we always buy locally. We did that again, but she wasn't happy about it. She was doing the same thing for T-shirts, sound equipment for the dance, everything. Usually, we didn't fight her on it. We all have jobs and lives and it seemed Vicki lived for the Winter Carnival and just was so much more passionate about it. When Esi started asking questions about the finances, Vicki got upset."

"When was this?"

"Our last meeting before Christmas."

"So just a week or two before Esi went to the deputy mayor."

"Yeah. And you know how far she got with him."

Penny knew the deputy mayor had politely stonewalled Esi, enough that it had made her even more curious and ready to dig deeper into the financials. What was still unclear was whether Vicki really was skimming off the Winter Carnival's budget. And if she was, whether that got her killed.

Penny thanked Tammy for the talk and offered an apology for her insinuations about Roger. She still found it hard to believe that a little community carnival could have led to murder, but it was the only thread she had to pull.

As she glanced at Tammy tidying up her gear in her locker, she thought about the deputy chief's assertion that firefighting was in her blood. There was a moment, in the radio room with Mason Arthur when he was introducing her to the arriving crew of firefighters, that she felt the sense of belonging that must come with what they did. The work of a dedicated team, helping people on their worst days. They had tried to help Vicki, but it had been too late for her.

"Tammy, can I get your phone number?"

"In case you change your mind about applying? Sure," she said as she folded the tops of her bunker pants over her boots and tucked the straps to the sides.

"Actually, I was hoping I could ask you about what happens at the meeting tonight."

Sixteen

The Truitt home was one of the most elaborate in Shells Harbour. It once belonged to a prominent fishing family before their descendants moved to Boston. Dr. Truitt bought it and moved in with his bride, Vicki. She was generally thought of as the luckiest lady in Shells Harbour for landing Roger Truitt when he arrived as the hospital's new emergency room physician almost a decade earlier.

Now the beautiful home was being readied for Vicki's memorial. Penny arrived as Arlene arranged flowers in the front hall and guided a caterer toward the kitchen with plates of finger food.

As Arlene splayed nibbles on serving trays laid out atop a marble-stone centre island in the stainless-steel kitchen, she told Penny about Vicki's life since high school.

"She had been at the Twisted Anchor for a while, waiting tables and pouring beer. She seemed to like it. We were a lot closer back then." Arlene paused for a moment and Penny stayed quiet, not wanting to rush her friend.

"I'd go see her at work a lot. I was there the night Roger first came in. Everyone knew about him, of course, the new young doctor in town. I knew there were folks who wondered why he went after my sister, but she was different. She was happy, independent. She rented the room above the Jungle Cafe and had put all the stuff with Panzer behind her. My sister was even thinking about going to college."

"What did she want to study?"

"History, actually. She loved digging into old stuff. Vicki could tell you the entire story of Shells Harbour if you wanted to listen. She wanted to write books, maybe teach," Arlene said. "She was even working on our family history at one point. But when she became the doctor's wife, that was it. Don't get me wrong, she loved her husband. But when they got married, and she got pregnant with Jared almost right away, the college plans went out the window."

Arlene glanced around the Truitt kitchen and lowered her voice.

"Roger married Vicki knowing the talk that had gone around when she worked at Panzer's. I didn't think it bothered him, but I wonder if he wanted my sister as a trophy wife with two perfect little kids."

A shriek from deep inside the house pierced the air, startling Penny.

"Becky," Arlene sighed and went off in search of the noise as it expanded into a deep wail. Penny trailed behind, taking in the screaming as well as the surroundings. The house was immaculate. Even if Vicki had cleaning help, it would have been a constant effort to keep it tidy with the kids and her busy life.

Arlene mounted the stairs and Penny followed her down a hallway laid with wide-plank timbers before turning to what had to be a child's room. It was an assault of pink. Carpet, walls, plush toys and dollhouses were all coloured in bright bubblegum and in the centre, red-faced Becky stood in an eight-year-old rage, facing off with her brother Jared. The fight appeared to be over wearing a frilly dress to her mother's memorial.

Arlene knelt to soothe the girl, and Penny marvelled at her friend's deep well of caring. Or maybe it was all part of how she was trying to cope. At some point, Penny thought, Arlene's shock will turn to grief and when it does, Penny vowed to be there for Arlene.

For now, though, Penny backed away from the family as the chime of the doorbell echoed through the heritage home. "I can get that." She moved out of the sea of pink and started back down the hall. From a different angle, Penny could see beyond the staircase they'd climbed and to the end of the hall, where the door to the master bedroom was open.

Roger sat on the edge of the bed. Whatever he registered of the world around him — the children crying, the guests gathering — he wasn't showing. Penny thought for a moment that she might speak to him, but the persistent doorbell called her away, and she left Roger alone.

At the front door, Penny came face-to-face with Erin Riggings and a man with shaggy, greying hair and a belly that threatened the buttons on his beige shirt. Erin was clearly surprised to see Penny behind the Truitt door, but she attempted to hide it and bustled her way into the home without introducing the companion that Penny took to be her husband, Ward.

The hospital's board came for the memorial, as well as doctors and nurses and other workers. One by one, they approached Roger with gentle concern and condolences when he emerged from the bedroom in a dark blue suit and cornflower tie. The members of the Winter Carnival board also arrived. Tammy greeted Penny with quiet warmth. Erin seemed to hover around everyone, picking snacks off catered trays. Each time Penny caught sight of her, she was on the edge of another group, listening in to the conversation. Sheila arrived with Esi, and Jacob and Paul came together.

Jacob appeared at Penny's elbow as she chatted with Jared's hockey coach, who was also a frequent customer at Brittle Pages.

"Arlene asked for your help in the kitchen," Jacob said, and Penny excused herself from the conversation.

Penny and Jacob found their old friend stirring a mug of steaming coffee poured from a fresh pot. She'd succeeded in getting Becky dressed, compromising on a less frilly outfit. An electronic tablet occupied the child in a corner of the living room while adults mingled around her.

"That little girl doesn't have a clue what to make of all this," Arlene said, looking into the mug. Penny filled Jacob in on the tantrum from earlier about her outfit.

"Chris does that too," Jacob said. "One day he'll just decide he hates his favourite t-shirt, or he'll refuse to wear socks."

Penny looked at Jacob. "I'd love to see you stand off with a seven-year-old having a tantrum."

"Yeah, he's a great kid, but don't try to get him anywhere quickly. It'll be jacket on, mitts off. Hat on the floor, boots on the wrong feet. Every morning."

"Vicki would do everything for Becky," Arlene said. "She spoiled her little princess and she wasn't shy about it. I told her it would backfire when Becky became a teenager. Now I'll never get to say I told you so," Arlene said with a chuckle. But she looked at Penny and Jacob with actual tears in her eyes. "I don't know what Roger's going to do with those kids."

Penny went to her side and ran her arm around Arlene's shoulders. Jacob slid a box of tissues off the top of the refrigerator and passed it to her. Arlene wiped her eyes and inhaled deeply to steady herself.

"Do you have anything new?"

Jacob and Penny told Arlene about meeting Coleridge Coleman at his home and his insistence that he didn't know Vicki.

"What about my grandfather's truck?"

"It's likely that someone tried to steal it. Probably unrelated to anything else going on. A couple teenagers trying their luck," Jacob said.

"I should have sold that truck," Arlene said. "I don't know why I just let it sit there. We got my grandmother moved into Lazy Pines a few years ago. There was a part of me that thought I might give it to Zach when he turned 16, but it probably wasn't fit for even a teenager to run around in."

Jacob hesitated for a moment, looking between Penny and Arlene. "There's one more thing you should know about Vicki. Dr. Alash, the medical examiner, said she didn't die in the fire."

"She didn't? What do you mean?"

"It looks like she had a wound that would have been severe enough to cause her death before the fire," Jacob said. Arlene looked at him for a moment, unblinking. Then her eyes narrowed.

"Who did it to her? Tell me, Jacob."

"I don't know that yet, I promise you. If I did, I'd tell the police and they'd be in handcuffs."

Arlene shrank back against the island in the middle of the kitchen.

Penny stood closer to her and glanced at Jacob, who leaned across the island to create a small, intimate triangle.

"We have a lot of questions about what happened to Vicki, but I am beginning to think it had something to do with the directors of the Winter Carnival."

"The board?" Arlene said, wiping her eyes again with the tissue. "Was something going on with them?"

"We're not sure," Jacob said. "Penny's been talking to some people, and it sounds like there might have been financial problems."

Arlene looked at her friends.

"Something shifted in Vicki last fall, when the carnival board planning meetings started. She was more hateful than usual. Complaining about everything and everybody," Arlene said. "I wondered if something was going on. She would chew over every little thing, but then she'd be at my door asking for a favour. Like the day before she died."

"She was? What did she want?"

"She wanted Jared to walk home with Zach after school and then go to hockey practice with us. Vicki had a fitting for her carnival dance dress."

"Do you know where that was?"

"That would have been with Jess," Jacob said. "She made Vicki's dress every year."

Penny raised her eyebrows at Jacob.

"My ex, Jess Anderson. She started her dress shop, Swishes, a year before Chris was born. Vicki would bring her ideas and they would have a bunch of meetings about it before the thing was done. Sometimes Jess needed me to pick Chris up early since Vicki was coming in for a fitting."

"You're right," Arlene said. "Most people were content to buy something from off the rack, but Vicki needed a unique dress. Something that no one else would have."

"Cost me a pretty penny, too."

The trio turned in unison to see Roger Truitt enter the kitchen and immediately clutch at the knot on his tie to loosen it. "But she wanted to be the belle of the ball," he said. "I gave her a hard time about the dresses, but she always looked beautiful. Not that I ever told her that."

He seemed like he was talking to himself more than the three of them. Penny glanced at Jacob, who met her gaze with his own look of concern. And then, Roger was out of the reverie and was back to being the polite host, embracing Arlene, greeting Jacob and introducing himself to Penny. "Thank you all for coming," he said, tightening the knot again.

Arlene watched him until she was certain he was far down the hall, mingling with other guests and out of earshot.

"Roger's exhausted. I better run interference for him." Arlene turned to leave the kitchen. Before she got to the hallway, she paused. "Please guys, don't give up. I think about Vicki there, in Coleridge's trailer, and I just, it's like I can't breathe," Arlene said, clutching the frame in the doorway with a tight grip. "I need to know what happened."

Penny went to Arlene and hugged her. "We're not going to stop," she vowed, hoping her tone gave Arlene confidence.

After Arlene left the kitchen, Penny met Jacob's worried look. Through a window over the polished stainless-steel sink, she noticed the forecasted snow had started to fall in heavy flakes. That would do enough to wrap up Vicki's memorial soon.

"That's going to make a mess," Jacob said as Penny realized he'd appeared behind her to look out of the same window. "Could be busy tonight with calls."

Penny looked back at her old friend. Worry lines marked his forehead, wrinkles that she knew would only deepen over time. With every storm and every squeal of the pager.

"Jacob, am I in over my head here? How can we possibly find out what happened to Vicki?"

"I don't know, Pen," he said. "I'd say leave it to the police, but they haven't returned even one of my phone calls."

Penny shook her head. "They're not going to give Arlene any answers," she said. "I might have no idea what I'm doing, but at least I'm doing something."

Seventeen

The snow fell, covering Shells Harbour with white insulation. Penny spent the rest of the memorial fielding questions from guests surprised to see her back in town. She also spent time simply listening to the talk that flowed through the Truitt home. There was an undercurrent of unease in the community. Arlene wasn't the only one who wanted to know how a young mother, a doctor's wife, ended up dead in Coleridge Coleman's trailer.

Penny overheard speculation about Coleridge being Vicki's secret lover, her drug dealer, or a cousin from away who'd come to cause trouble. There was a general buzz about the responsibility of the man who lived at the edge of Shells Harbour for the crime.

She doubted the truth of any scrap of the gossip and struggled to reconcile the broken man she'd met with the idea that he could be a killer. And even though she shared her doubts with Jacob about solving the murder, there was one step she could take in retracing Vicki's movements during the last few days of her life. And that meant a visit with Jacob's ex-girlfriend.

Swishes, the dress shop, was tucked on the ground floor of a newer building a few blocks away from Brittle Pages. A pet store shared half the building, and apartments were tucked upstairs. Displays of mannequins in sequin-studded and lace dresses for weddings and dances lined the window now edged with an inch of snow.

Penny pulled open the handle and breathed in Swishes' scent of perfumed roses, the melted-wax type that was probably plugged into a wall socket somewhere in the cozy shop. Jess Anderson glanced up from her position behind an elaborate sewing table. A lock of straight red hair had become loose from her bun and she tucked it behind her ear.

"Hi there, can I help you?"

Penny took a breath. She wanted to manage the conversation with Jess with more tact than she had with Tammy Johnson.

"Hi Jess, I'm not sure if you remember me. Penny Pintz."

Penny pulled her crimson knit cap off her head and smoothed her brown hair around her jacket collar. Jess looked at Penny closely.

"Of course, yes, you were a year ahead of me, right?"

"That's right. Remember a few nights around the gravel pit on Outcrop Road?" Penny wasn't sure if she should remind Jess of her friendship with Jacob, although it seemed the exes were amicable. Jess laughed.

"That feels like a million years ago. I never knew about the pit until the first time Jacob brought me there."

"And none of us would have known about it if it weren't for Arlene Barkson. Right down the road from her grandparents' house."

Jess's smile faded. "Oh my, Arlene. How is she holding up?"

"I suppose as well as you might expect."

Jess turned her back to Penny and smoothed a bolt of cloth stacked on a cutting counter. "And those poor children. My son, Chris, is in school with Becky and Jared."

"We're really all still wrapping our heads around it. Actually, that's why I'm here," Penny said. "Arlene told me you were making Vicki's dress for the Winter Carnival ball."

"Yes, that's right. She was just here. The day before the fire."

Jess moved out from behind the counter and Penny saw the woman was wearing a handmade dress with a long burgundy skirt patterned with yellow dandelions. For a moment, Penny imagined Jess with Jacob, arms intertwined, holding a younger Chris as a happy family. Jess in a flowing dress and loose knit sweater, Jacob in his navy-blue fire uniform.

I missed so much while I was in Toronto, she thought. Jacob and

Arlene lived entire lives that I know nothing about, and they know nothing about mine. She shook her head to clear the image.

"It's hard to believe," Jess said. "She was perfectly fine when she came in, giddy almost. I showed her the dress, and she tried it on for a fitting."

"Which one was it?"

"I have it right here." Jess turned to a rack of dresses and plucked out a gown that she laid out on her sewing table. Penny ran her fingers along the silky blue fabric, the same cornflower shade as the tie Roger wore during the memorial. Penny wondered if that was Vicki's favourite colour. The stitched beadwork glinted. The doctor's wife would have looked gorgeous in it, with her blond hair styled up. She would have shone in the spotlights that transform the Shells Harbour Community Centre into a ballroom.

"I'm quite proud of this one. The best I've done for Vicki yet." Jess plucked at an invisible speck on a shoulder strap.

"What did Vicki say about it?"

"She loved it. A lot," Jess added for emphasis. "I've made dresses for weddings, for proms, I've done all of it. She was possibly the most excited person to try on one of my designs."

"I can understand why. It's a gorgeous dress."

"It was a lot of work, yes." Jess let her words trail. She pulled the dress off the table and slipped its shoulders back on the hanger. "I don't know what to do with it now."

"Vicki would have looked beautiful in it," Penny said, trying to urge the conversation on.

"She did. And she couldn't wait to be seen in it. She had me take pictures with her phone when she was trying it on."

"Is that so? She probably sent them to Roger."

Jess looked at the dress and turned her back to Penny.

"I'm not sure if she wanted the pictures for her husband."

"What do you mean?"

"When I had her phone, a text message popped up. It said, 'meet me at the place I told you about, tomorrow morning'."

"That seems strange. Do you know who it was from?"

Jess shook her head and glanced to the side, where Penny saw two teenage girls looking at a sparkling pink dress on a mannequin in the window. One of them snapped a picture of it with her phone before they moved down the street. For a moment, Penny remembered shopping for prom dresses with Arlene at the mall in Oaktown. Vicki tagged along that rainy Saturday where they spent more time in the mall's food court than dress shopping. Taking Vicki was the only way Arlene got permission to borrow her mother's Ford Escort, but the younger girl entertained them with jokes and coffee refills.

"I'm not sure," Jess said. "There was no name, just a phone number. I told her she was getting a message and handed her phone back."

"How did she react?"

"She wasn't smiling anymore, that's for sure," Jess said with a shrug. "She paid me for the dress and asked me to have the last alterations done by today."

Penny thanked Jess and left the dress shop with one more thought about the life Jacob and Jess might have had, and one last glance at the ball gown. As she stepped onto the street, she paused in the warm winter sun. She tried to imagine Vicki in the dress as a grown woman. But Penny was stuck on the memory of her years earlier, trailing them through the mall, passing along gossip about which couples held hands in line for the movie theatre and who snuck cigarettes outside in the parking lot.

Penny remembered the girl Vicki was then, ready with a smile, her blond hair tied in a messy ponytail, wearing ripped jeans and her junior high school sweatshirt.

That was the girl who lived in Penny's memory. A memory that had grown clouded, dark in the days since her death. Time and circumstance changed people, Penny knew, and Vicki's adulthood might have brought secrets that backed her into a corner.

Penny was about to pull away from the curbside parking spot she'd snagged outside Swishes when she noticed a yellow slip of paper tucked underneath a windshield wiper.

Penny groaned as she reached around to pluck the paper through her opened window. The ticket had the blue and white logo of the Shells Harbour Police Department. Penny had slipped coins into the meter at the curb before entering Jess's shop and as she got out of her car, she could see that the timer hadn't expired yet.

She looked up the road and saw a man dressed in blue, with an SHPD flash on his shoulder and a yellow booklet in his hand.

"Excuse me!" She called to the officer, who was now a few cars up the road. "You wrote me a ticket, but my meter hasn't expired yet."

The officer glanced up from the parking meter he was reading and eyed Penny. He was young; she guessed mid-twenties, with brown eyes and a narrow chin that he attempted to cover with a patchy beard.

"Your ticket's not for a meter violation, ma'am," the officer said. "Your out of province plates are expired."

Penny brought her hand to her forehead and exhaled. She had put off getting a local license plate, as if committing to a Nova Scotia registration was a step too far in declaring her residency. She looked at the ticket wrinkled in her hand and nodded slightly.

"That was silly of me," she said to the officer. "I moved back here at Christmas and forgot to switch my plates over."

The police officer tucked the booklet of unwritten violations back into the pocket of his police vest.

"Well, let this be a lesson," he said as he began to walk down the block. "We're always keeping an eye on this town."

Penny looked at the yellow paper crumpled in her hand and the retreating police officer. His words echoed in her mind and as he moved further away, without glancing at any of the other parked cars that lined the curb. Penny noticed hers was the only one ticketed.

Eighteen

"Tell me I'm being paranoid," Penny said. "Tell me I've read too many detective books."

Sheila adjusted a loose shoulder of her striped blouse and looked at Penny with a frown. Paul folded his arms and leaned against the fiction stack near the entrance to the kitchen at Brittle Pages.

"Describe him for me," he asked. Penny detailed as much as she could about the police officer.

"He didn't sign the ticket, so I don't know what his name is."

"That's not hard to figure out. Sounds like it's the fellow who joined the force a few years back, kid from up Cape Breton," Paul said. "Think his name is Jimmy, or Johnny, or something."

"It's Wally," Sheila said. "Wally McPhee. I remember when the department hired him, they put his picture in the paper. He's on this street a lot, giving out tickets. It might have just been about your plates, Pen."

"I hope you're right, but there was something about the way he spoke to me. Like it was a warning."

Penny pulled her phone out of her pocket and looked up McPhee's profile on social media. "For a cop, he's got a pretty public profile. It says he's in a relationship with Ria Cranson. Why is that name familiar?"

"That would be the youngest daughter of our deputy mayor," Paul said.

"The man who doesn't want Esi to look into the weird financial stuff going on with the carnival committee?" Penny crossed her arms and leaned against the doorway that led into the bookstore's supply closet. "Now tell me I'm just paranoid."

Paul glanced at Sheila, whose eyes had narrowed. "I don't think you have a reason to be concerned for your safety though," he said, as much to Penny as to her aunt. "In fact, it was probably just a coincidence. You have out-of-province plates, so McPhee might have just been a bit nimby."

"A bit what?" Penny asked.

"Nimby," Paul repeated. "N-I-M-B-Y. Not in my backyard."

Penny groaned. "Right, that welcoming small-town sentiment." She wondered if Paul really felt like she was overthinking McPhee's comment, or if he was simply reassuring her, and by extension, Sheila. He changed the subject.

"I've been meaning to ask you, why were you and Jacob looking into the Barkson house the other day when we had the truck fire there?"

Penny looked between her aunt and the deputy fire chief. Jacob already thought she was imagining the movement she had seen in the hallway at Arlene's grandparents' house. She decided not to add to her friend's worries at the memorial by mentioning it then.

"I haven't told Arlene this, but I thought I saw something inside the house," Penny said. "I tried the door, and it was locked up tight. Jacob thought I was seeing things."

"I don't think anyone has stepped foot in that old place in some time," Paul said.

"That's what Jacob said too. But I saw something moving. And how could Albert's old truck just catch on fire like that?"

"I'd bet someone was trying to jump it. Maybe to steal." Paul said. "Set off a few too many sparks in that old beast."

"If someone did set it on fire, do you think they would have hid inside the house? Stayed right there?" Sheila asked Penny skeptically. "That place is probably full of cracks and holes for the wind to slip in."

"What else have you found out?" Paul asked. Penny dropped the subject of what she saw in the house, even though she wasn't convinced the flutter was caused by a draft. She gave them a run-down of her conversation with Jess Anderson, with Vicki being summoned in an anonymous text message to a meeting spot, and her behaviour about it.

"I want to find out what the carnival committee decided last night," Penny said, looking at Sheila. "Have you heard from Esi?" Her aunt shook her head.

"She had to take Kofi into the hospital to get the cast off his arm early this morning," Sheila explained. "He got a bad sprain in hockey last month. It was actually Vicki who took him to the emergency room, because Esi had missed that game. Sat with him until she could get there."

"Going by the phone message that Jess told you about, do you think there might be a more obvious answer here?" Paul asked.

"What do you mean?"

"Well, if she was telling Roger about her dress, she'd probably have his name saved in her phone, not just a number. And he would have just seen the outfit at home or at the ball, not in some special meeting place."

Penny looked at him closely and cocked her head to the right. Paul was showing a curiosity about her investigation that she didn't know he had. "Detective Deputy Chief, what are you saying?"

He shrugged. "Maybe I'm the one who reads too many books, but it sounds to me like Vicki might have been having an affair."

"I find that hard to believe," Sheila said. Penny knew her aunt wanted to only see the good in a person, and struggled to acknowledge the possibility of darker parts. "She seemed very happy, settled in her life."

"Maybe that's it. She was young when she got married and became a mother. Maybe she felt stifled by life as a doctor's wife," Penny suggested. "Arlene told me Vicki had been especially hateful lately. Maybe the guilt of cheating was getting to her."

"But I thought this whole thing was over money. And the Winter Carnival board audit," Sheila said.

"What if it's all connected? Maybe Vicki was trying to find a way to ferret away cash to leave her husband."

Sheila raised a skeptical eyebrow. "I knew I shouldn't have let you watch all those soap operas after school."

Penny pushed aside the coffee mug Sheila had placed on the cash counter of the bookstore. Her aunt had worked hard to make the shop seem like a casual, cozy place and Penny knew the gossip of an affair was not what Sheila wanted aired in Brittle Pages. But Penny still cast her mind to Vicki, and she wondered what Roger's life was like with her. If she was cheating on him, violating his trust, Penny wondered if he could have damaged her in return.

"I know it might sound far-fetched, but desperation and anger can push a person," Penny said. "And maybe I'm wrong, but what if I'm not? No one else has any idea why Vicki was killed. And the police don't seem to be doing much, other than handing out tickets for expired plates. They haven't even spoken to Arlene yet."

"So, what do you do next?" Paul asked. Penny was happy to see the senior firefighter interested in her amateur investigation.

"Actually, I need to talk to Tammy Johnson," she said. "Last night's Winter Carnival meeting was going to be about how to carry on without Vicki."

"I heard they're planning a tribute," Paul said. "But Tammy can tell you about that."

Penny nodded. "And after I talk to her, I think I need to find Roger."

"Be careful," Sheila said. "You remember how he was at the memorial? He wasn't in a good frame of mind then. And he might not be much better now to be questioned about his marriage, especially by a stranger who has no authority to be asking." Sheila gave Penny a pointed look that was sharp enough to make Penny avert her eyes after a moment. Sheila gathered her oversized canvas market bag filled with books and papers, but paused. Penny could tell her aunt was thinking about something.

"If that McPhee fellow is watching you, it could be connected to Roger," Sheila said. "It was Lowell Cranson that recruited him here when we had a doctor shortage at the hospital."

Paul nodded. "I was the deputy head of administration then," he said. "Cranson was very proud of himself when Roger Truitt moved to Shells Harbour and we always wondered what sort of promises Cranson made."

"Promises?"

"Every town in this province needs doctors, so recruitment is quite competitive. You hear stories of kickbacks, extra bonuses. I didn't see any evidence of it on the hospital's records, but the way Cranson operates, I might never know."

"Did you ever get any complaints about Roger?"

Paul shook his head. "Roger is a fine doctor. People said he'd work through his patients quickly, but that was the expectation in the emergency room. He'd see dozens of people each day."

"Maybe there's a reason he'd work so quickly," Penny said, her speculation running fast. "What if he's finding his way into the hospital sample closet? Writing his own prescriptions or something? Maybe that's why Vicki was cheating."

Sheila gripped her tote bag tighter and turned her brown eyes firmly to her niece.

"Penny, take a breath. I strongly suggest you don't go around town saying things like that. If you really want to find out what happened to Vicki, accusing her of infidelity and her husband of being a drug addict is a fast way to get doors closed in your face. Roger Truitt has a lot of respect in this town. He's saved lives here."

"You're right," Penny said, nodding and exhaling. She had gotten too far ahead of herself. "I'll be more tactful."

Sheila swung her bulging bag around and knocked off a small stack of paperbacks that Penny would spend her afternoon cataloging. Paul bent to pick them up at the same moment Sheila did. The heavy bag slid off her shoulder and into Paul's bent back, eliciting a grunt.

"I'm so sorry," Sheila said, cringing as she stood. She put her hand on Paul's arm as he straightened, the spilled books forgotten on the floor. Penny watched the scene with curiosity as Sheila moved her hand to the spot where her bag collided with Paul's back.

"I'll get those," Penny said, moving from behind the counter to the front to collect the paperbacks. "I think you owe Paul a coffee for that, Sheila."

Paul chuckled. "Oh, I'm alright, had much worse than that bump into me at fire calls." Still, Penny was certain she detected a glimmer in his eyes at her suggestion.

"I carry way too much stuff around, and I'm a bit clumsy," Sheila said.

"Don't I know it. Gym class," Paul said. "The rope ladder." Sheila was quiet for a moment, and Penny could tell she was searching her memory. A wide smile soon broke out on her face, crinkling the corners of her eyes.

"You mean when I tried to climb the ladder, and I fell?"

"And you landed right on top of me, cause I was your spotter," Paul said, laughing harder. Penny felt like she was watching them in high school as Sheila leaned into Paul.

"That wasn't clumsiness," Sheila said. "Tommy White had climbed before me, and he got the rope sweaty. I was so grossed out that I let go."

"And I got your knee in my nose," Paul said. "That was a lot of blood."

"That wasn't the first time I got yelled at in gym class. Old Mr. Nickerson was not a fan of my athletic inability."

"Did you know his son teaches gym now?"

"Well, I certainly hope he's nicer to the kids than his father was," Sheila said. "I blame Nickerson for my fear of organized sports."

"You wouldn't be the only Shells Harbour High survivor to say that," Paul said. "Why don't I walk you out? Make sure you handle the curb safely."

Penny watched the pair leave and for a moment her thoughts weren't swirling around Vicki Truitt's death. Her aunt had dated a few men since her divorce. No relationship had lasted longer than a year or two and Sheila had settled into her single life with her career and a full calendar of friendships and community volunteering. But Penny had started to hope the deputy chief might bring a different ending to her aunt's story.

Nineteen

The Lazy Pines parking lot looked at first glance like any other medium-sized brown brick apartment building. But the wide wheelchair ramp at the front entrance was a hint about the tenants who lived inside. Arlene looked up at the building and sighed.

"I wanted her to come live with me, but Tim thought it would be too much," she said. "Zach was little. We were thinking back then we'd try for another one. Obviously, that never happened. Vicki thought she'd be better off here. We arrange for groceries, and they make her some meals and have social events. But I still wish I'd fought harder to have her with me."

Arlene tapped a code into a keypad, and an electronic lock was released on the door. She led Penny down a hallway lit with warm fluorescent fixtures and laid with an orange and beige carpet that was trendy a few decades past. She paused in front of room 116 and rapped her knuckles on the door.

From inside the apartment, a shaky but still strong voice called them inside. Mary Barkson was more stooped than Penny remembered, leaning her left hand on a chipped veneer kitchen table for support as she fiddled with a spread of cookies and tea.

Arlene hugged her grandmother, and Penny stepped forward.

"Mrs. Barkson, it's so lovely to see you," she said, raising her arms for a hug. Mary Barkson clutched her hands with a firm grip before pulling Penny in.

"None of that Mrs. Barkson nonsense. You're a grown-up now Penny, you call me Mary." Penny smiled and wrapped Mary in a hug, placing her hands gently on soft, slim shoulders. In return, Mary gave her a squeeze and chided her for not visiting sooner.

"I heard you were back in town. And this is the first time I'm seeing you," Mary said, shaking her head. "How's Sheila and her little bookstore?"

Penny thought of Sheila and Paul and their gentle teasing earlier at Brittle Pages. Her aunt was content in a way that gave Penny a quiet joy. "She's doing well, thank you." They settled at the table with cookies to nibble and the television humming an American talk show in the living room of the small, open-concept apartment.

The cloud would descend with the second cup of tea, after talking of how Zach was doing in school and how Arlene was getting on as a single mother. Mary asked about Penny's parents.

"They're still out west," she replied simply. "Last I spoke to mom, anyway. Which was about six months ago."

Mary looked at Penny closely and nodded. She shifted her attention back to her granddaughter.

"How are Roger and the children holding up?"

"Roger's back at the hospital already. He said he couldn't just sit home and do nothing," Arlene said. "Jared's been over at the house with Zach almost every day. They play their video games and shoot hockey pucks outside."

Mary's usually soft face set hard in a grimace. "And the little one?"

Arlene shook her head, and for a moment, her words didn't come. Penny saw tears in Arlene's eyes and put her hand on her friend's back for comfort.

"Becky's so much like her mother. You remember how stubborn Vicki was? Becky's exactly like that. I know she and Vicki were butting heads and she's doing the same thing to Roger now, but so much worse. I don't know what's going to become of that girl."

"I'd like to see the children, if I may," Mary said.

"Of course. How about this weekend? We'll come for a visit. Jared will probably be at my house anyway and if Roger's working, I'll look after Becky, too."

Mary shook her head, and Penny watched as she extended a hand to rip a tissue from the box on the table. She wiped her eyes and Penny saw years of sadness deep in them. Mary Barkson had a life pockmarked by grief. Arlene and Vicki's mother, Mary's daughter, had died from cancer when they were all in high school. The agony of that time had marked their teenage years and Vicki's anger turned into darkness for a period. Their parents had already separated, and the girls lived full time with their mother. When she died, they lost not only their parent, but their home as well.

Vicki moved in with their father, a long-haul trucker who made runs across Canada and into America that would have him away from home for days on end. Arlene lived with Mary and Albert for her last year of high school, but Vicki took full advantage of her father's absence. Penny and Arlene would often get to school on a Monday morning and hear stories about Vicki's parties, which usually ended by being broken up by town police. But she was 16, and there was food in the house and a father present occasionally, so the social worker who responded to neighbours' complaints about a child living alone could do little about the situation.

Penny was a regular at the Barkson house on Outcrop Road, even before Arlene moved in. As Vicki spiralled through her teenage years, Mary kept the door to the old house open and a spare bed made up for nights when Vicki didn't want to be alone. Mary wanted to keep close to the family she still had. And now she'd have to figure out how to do the same with her great-grandchildren.

Mary leaned back in the wooden dining chair and rubbed a hand over her face. Her short, grey-white hair was cut with wisps that flicked out around her ears and her beige cable-knit sweater was loose on a frame that had lost weight since Penny had seen her.

"I hate to ask this, but things just don't make sense to me," Mary said after a moment. "What on earth was Vicki doing at that trailer?"

Arlene looked toward Penny, who spoke first.

"Actually, that's a mystery to us as well," she said. "I've been helping the fire department with their investigation and so far, it seems like Vicki was living her life as she normally would have been. She was knee-deep in planning the Winter Carnival and running the kids all over the place."

"The carnival? I thought she was quitting that," Mary said.

Penny and Arlene exchanged a glance. From everything Penny had heard, Vicki was the driving force behind the planning committee and no one she'd spoken to had even hinted about her leaving.

"What makes you say that, Mary?"

"She was here the other week, dropping off a few things from the drugstore for me. I knew it was carnival season, so I asked her and she said she was done with it. Didn't want to talk much more, you know how she can get. Could get," Mary said, correcting herself to put Vicki in the past tense.

"You're the first person I've heard that from," Penny said.

But Mary nodded to show the women she was sure of what she was saying. Penny had no reason to doubt. Her mind seemed as sharp as it had ever been.

"She told me she had other projects she was working on. She'd been coming here all winter, asking all kinds of questions about the family," Mary said, glancing at Arlene. "I'm surprised you didn't know."

Arlene cleared her throat and took a sip of her tea. "Vicki and I had our issues, as you know, Grandma. And we hadn't been as close as I'd have liked in these last few years."

Mary's eyebrows knitted together, as if she was struggling to answer a tricky question in the crossword puzzles she liked to play. She coughed, her lungs rattling deep within her chest with a force that started Penny. With a shaky hand, Mary reached into a pocket of her sweater and pulled out an inhaler, drawing a deep breath of medication into her body. After a few long moments with Arlene by her side, rubbing her back, she calmed down and accepted the glass of water Penny had drawn for her.

"Sorry girls," she said with a rasp. "This damn winter has settled into my bones."

But Penny knew a cough like that had nothing to do with the season. Behind Mary's back, Arlene looked at Penny and shook her head. Arlene took her seat again and Mary's breathing normalized with the help of the inhaler. After a moment, she was ready to talk again.

"What was Vicki curious about?" Penny asked.

"She was keen to fill in some branches on the family tree," Mary said. "She had been doing the genealogy and was looking for what I could remember about some of your grandfather's relations. Not much, as it turned out, but we had fun trying to connect the dots. She was still at it, far as I know. I thought it was nice. She had a little hobby for herself."

Mary paused and Penny felt something unsaid lingering in the dry air of the Lazy Pines apartment, mingling with the light scent of a lemon floor cleaner. Mary had more to say. But when she looked up from the tissue that she had knotted between her fingers, something else was on her mind, and the moment passed.

"I'd like you to think about what you want to do about that old house."

Penny looked at Arlene, who was staring into the bottom of her empty teacup. Mary had hit a nerve, and it was a long moment before Arlene spoke.

"Vicki and I never agreed on what to do with it," Arlene said. "She hung on so tight, even though she made the choice to go live with dad, and not us, after mom died."

Arlene reached out to cover the tight fist Mary had made.

"What do you want to do, Gram?"

Mary was still for a moment. Penny could see her energy fade and the breaths she took sounded slightly laboured.

"Let's just get through the winter," she said finally. "Everything will look different in the spring."

Arlene nodded. Penny was quietly pleased, since she knew Arlene had too much on her plate, too many big decisions and bigger devastations she was already managing. There would be time, later, to figure out the fate of the old house on Outcrop Road.

Penny gathered the empty teacups and gave them a quick wash in the sink while Arlene and her grandmother embraced.

They left Mary settled in her easy chair, a crossword at her side and another talk show humming away on the television. Penny saw how tightly Arlene hugged her. When they left, Arlene clutched the strap of her purse and hurried along the hallway, as if she was trying to escape Lazy Pines.

"Arlene, what is it?" Penny finally asked when they emerged in the chilly daylight of the parking lot.

"She's sick, Penny. Her lungs are destroyed, all those years of breathing in Grandpa Albert's smoke. It's going to kill her."

"I'm so sorry," Penny said.

"And she brings up that damn house." Arlene threw her hands in the air. "We should have sold it years ago. Vicki had it valued once. I never quite believed it, but she said we'd be looking at more than a million for it. She'd had a few developers come in and tell her that with the land associated with the house and the demand from a lot of foreigners wanting to build on the ocean, we could break it up into plots and sell each one."

"Why didn't you?"

Arlene sighed. "I just wasn't ready to let it go. It was more of a home to me than it ever was to Vicki, but she didn't get it. We did the vacation rental thing for a while and then we had a tenant in there, a woman who came to town to work at Tim's company for a time."

Arlene reached into her handbag to dig out her hat and gloves, and Penny did the same as a winter wind swirled around them. "And that was just a complete disaster."

"What happened with her?"

"She was a perfectly fine tenant until a few months ago, when she got fired and trashed the house as she left town," Arlene said, taking a sharp inhale of the cold air. "She got fired, and so did Tim, because they were having an affair. Which is against company policy anyway and was all the worse because she was in town to do an audit of Tim's department."

Penny felt her eyes widen, and she brought a hand to her mouth to cover her shocked face. "That's unbelievable," she said. "How could he be so stupid?"

"Oh, he's beyond stupid. And now he's being investigated by the company to see if he did something fraudulent. He denies it, but he also denied the affair until the company found emails between him and her. They used their bloody corporate emails to arrange their hook-ups, which were usually at the house."

"Did Vicki know about the affair?"

"She did, as did most people in Shells Harbour," Arlene said. "He's in the Lighthouse Motel now, in one of their long-term rooms and he's been working at the lumber mill, doing their books."

Arlene's phone chirped in her purse, and she reached into a pocket to retrieve it. With a glance at the screen, she let out a hard breath.

"It's the school. Roger put Becky back in today and she's having a meltdown. I assume he's not answering his phone and I'm on the contact sheet for her," Arlene said. "I'll go see if I can calm her down."

Penny watched her friend climb into her black SUV. Before Arlene pulled out of Lazy Pines, she rolled down her window.

"You really haven't spoken to Delphine in six months?"

"Actually, it's been more like two years," Penny said. "Maybe three." Arlene let out a wry chuckle.

"Glad to know I'm not the only one with a messed-up family," she said, glancing again at the screen of her phone. "I have to go. But can I ask you for a favour? You're already doing a lot for me, but I'm just swamped trying to help Roger with the kids."

"Of course. What do you need?"

"Jacob told me that whoever tried to steal my grandfather's truck might have because the house looks abandoned, since I kicked that woman out. I haven't been there this winter and I should go check on it."

"I'm happy to help," Penny said, feeling a vibration in her own pocket. She reached for her phone as Arlene thanked her and arranged to meet at the Barkson house later in the week. As Arlene pulled away from Lazy Pines, Penny looked at the screen on her phone.

I have to tell you what happened last night. Are you free today?

Whatever Tammy Johnson had to say, she wanted to do it in person.

Twenty

Penny piled a stack of books on the floor of Brittle Pages and sorted through the titles, arranging them according to where they'd be shelved. Sheila made sure her bookstore supported local writers, so authors and poets from across the coastal province featured prominently on her displays.

Books surrounded Penny's life and were the bedrock of her publishing career in Toronto. But, like the rest of her life in the city, her job hadn't gone the way she hoped. Penny glanced at the cover of a new book from an author who lived in a neighbouring county, a collection of folklore. It promised stories of haunted islands, shipwrecks and bad luck.

There was a story behind Vicki's death, she was sure. Penny ran around the information she'd collected in her head while she catalogued and shelved new books, waiting for Tammy. One cover, with a black-and-white photograph of the city of Halifax, caught her eye. The book that had as its subject the city at the turn of the century reminded Penny of Vicki's interest in local history. She might have written her own book, one day.

Penny hadn't known that Vicki had developed an interest in local lore, but then, she was coming to realize that she knew little about the people in the town where she was raised. Jacob was a father. Arlene's marriage was ending. Everyone in Shells Harbour had a story.

The burgundy door swung open and the bell over it chimed. Tammy stepped into the shop with an air of familiarity, and Penny wondered if she was a regular customer.

"Oh great, Sheila's got the new book in the Nemesis series," Tammy said. "I've been buying this for my stepdaughter. Although I read it first," she chuckled, plucking the paperback off the shelf and placing it on the counter. But Penny knew their transaction wasn't finished.

"Cup of coffee? I put a new pot on a few minutes ago," Penny offered. Tammy nodded and slid into the lounge chair in a corner near the kitchen entrance.

"Just a bit of cream."

After pouring their mugs, Penny settled on the stool behind the counter, and Tammy began. The carnival meeting had started late, she said, as they waited for Roger Truitt to arrive.

"We told him he didn't need to be there, but he insisted," she said. "He looked terrible. Like he hadn't slept or eaten a decent meal in days."

Penny nodded, remembering how Roger had seemed at Vicki's memorial. Exhausted and grieving.

"We decided to cancel the ball, but carry on with the rest of the carnival. By this point, plans are so far advanced that it would be more expensive to scrap it all," Tammy said. "We're going to hold a moment of silence at the puck-drop before the police-versus-fire hockey game."

The ball was usually the centerpiece of the carnival, and cancelling it wouldn't have been a simple decision, Penny knew.

"And then we got to the matter of the chairperson," Tammy said, taking a sip from her warm cup. "Erin thought she'd be a shoo-in. But it didn't work out like that for her."

"Really?"

Tammy nodded, with a smile that spread. She pulled the black winter toque embroidered with the logo for the fire department off her head and ran a hand over her blonde strands to smooth them back down.

"You're now looking at the carnival committee chair. Someone had to do it."

Penny smiled. "Congratulations," she said. "You seem like a good fit for a job like that."

"How so? Cause I'm pushy? A little loudmouthed?" Tammy said but had a grin on her face that was still crimson from the cold outside.

"No, not that," Penny said. "Certain. Assured. Good traits for a firefighter and for the chair of a community organization."

At that, Tammy laughed. "I suppose you're right," she said. "Thank you."

"What was Erin's response?"

"Safe to say she wasn't pleased. I thought she'd quit the committee on the spot, but she folded her arms and didn't say a peep for the rest of the meeting. Bolted as soon as it was done."

"And how did Roger react to all this?"

Tammy took another long sip of her coffee.

"He left not long after the vote. I dropped by his house after the meeting to see if he was alright," Tammy said. "He told me he didn't want visitors, but I made my way into the kitchen, and we had a cup of tea."

"How's he doing?"

"Not good, as I suspected. He's on autopilot. And he said he's been having trouble getting answers from the police," Tammy said. "He's not from here, and I tried to tell him that police, like a lot of things, work differently in small towns. Slower. Doesn't mean bad, just different."

Penny nodded. She wanted to tell Tammy about her run-in with Wally McPhee, but talking about Roger reminded her of something else.

"How long have you been on the carnival committee?"

"This is my sixth year."

"And Vicki had been on it for five years, so you must have known her well. What was she like?"

"I thought you knew her," Tammy said, eyebrows raised at Penny as she shifted in the lounge chair.

"Oh, I did, but I knew her as my best friend's little sister. As teenagers. Hanging around, wanting to butt in on what we were doing. You know how kids are," Penny said. "What was she like as an adult?"

"She knew what she wanted," Tammy said plainly. "Every year she had a vision for the carnival and every year, she made it happen."

"Was it difficult to work with her?" Penny asked, trying to be careful how she phrased her sentences.

Tammy paused and pushed herself out of Sheila's cozy chair. Penny watched as she stopped in front of a bookshelf of biographies of famous Canadians, with Margaret Atwood at her right shoulder and Maurice Richard on her left. She turned to face Penny.

"Yes, sometimes it was very difficult to work with her, I'll be honest. We excused a lot because the carnival was always amazing at the end, but getting there was another matter. Esi and I, we're pretty tough. Took a lot of Vicki's anger and got on with it because we wanted the community to have the carnival. There's nothing else here in the winter and we know how important it is."

Penny nodded but stayed silent to encourage Tammy to continue.

"Roger was there just to agree with his wife. He told me that one night at the curling rink when he'd had a few. But Vicki and Erin, they'd butt heads all the time. I was willing to do some of the extra work Vicki wanted. Stuff like we were talking about earlier. Getting multiple quotes on supplies we knew we'd buy locally, that type of thing."

Penny leaned her forearms on the counter and lightly twirled a small stack of bookmarks as she listened.

"Erin hated that. Hated the extra hoops Vicki wanted us to jump through. Erin's been on the committee since the carnival started back in the early 90s and she talks an awful lot about how things used to be," Tammy said. "If I'm honest, Vicki's way worked. Probably saved the committee a good amount of cash over the last few years."

"Saved money? I thought the committee was in trouble," Penny said. Tammy moved to the front window of the store and looked out on Barque Lane. Penny could tell she was reflecting on everything that had happened in the last few days, from Vicki's death to becoming chair of a committee that she considered quitting not too long ago.

"There were times that, when a supplier found out we were shopping around for quotes, they'd cut their prices to win the bid. That happened quite often, in fact, because everyone needed business in the winter," Tammy said. "I still think money was leaking out of the committee, but it wasn't because of Vicki. I need to spend more time with the numbers now that I'm the chair, but things aren't as I thought they were."

Penny took a long drink of her coffee and let Tammy's words settle over her. She'd followed the thread of the carnival committee's finances long enough that she was certain it would eventually lead to the reason Vicki died. If Tammy was right, Penny thought, I've been chasing my tail all over this town for a week.

"Did you have any reason to think that Vicki wanted to leave the carnival committee?"

Tammy chuckled. "Not one bit." But then she paused. "Now that you mention it, she seemed a little, I don't know, out of it lately. Distracted in meetings."

Before Penny could press for more details, a sharp chime sounded from within Tammy's shoulder bag. Once more, the Shells Harbour Fire Department was being summoned to someone's bad day.

"Gotta go." Tammy left the shop echoing with the jingle of the doorbell, and Penny confused about what she'd learned. Vicki wasn't taking money from the Winter Carnival. But she had still done something to make herself a target to her killer. She had told her grandmother she wanted to leave the committee, but Tammy only said Vicki had been distracted. It made no sense. Penny was no closer to finding answers for the people who cared about Vicki, including her husband, who sounded like he was just as frustrated with the police response as Arlene.

Penny took Tammy's half-full cup of coffee and tipped it out in the kitchen sink. She went back to cataloguing books, but her mind raced. What she'd learned about Vicki didn't add up, and Penny realized that Shells Harbour's secrets were proving to be more complex than she could have imagined.

She pulled her phone from the counter and typed a text to Arlene. There was one more person Penny needed to speak to, and Arlene had to be the one to open that door.

Twenty-One

"Dad! I can do it myself!"

An indignant child chirped behind Penny in the line at the Jungle Cafe. She glanced toward the noise and saw the boy fumbling with the zipper on a bulky winter coat. Jacob Bell stood next to him, with a slight smile sitting crookedly on his face. Some parents, Penny knew, reacted sternly when their children brushed them away. Jacob looked entertained.

Chris finally grasped the zipper tab with his mittened hands and tugged triumphantly, grinning.

"Good job buddy," Jacob said. "It's Friday, right?"

Chris nodded excitedly.

"And Friday is what?"

"Muffin day!"

"Well then, please take my spot in line for such an important event," Penny said, cutting into their conversation and gesturing in front of her. Chris gave her a narrow-eyed look of shyness and moved behind his father.

"Morning, Penny," Jacob said. "This is my boy, Chris. Chris, this is my friend Penny."

Penny held out a gloved hand to Chris. "I knew your dad when he was about your size," Penny said, offering a smile.

"Really?" Chris glanced at his father, as if trying to gauge the probability of him ever being a child. Jacob nodded. Chris stuck a mitten into Penny's hand and began unleashing a series of questions that made him temporarily forget about the chocolate chip muffin Jacob had just ordered, along with his coffee and Penny's latte.

"Are you a fireman like my dad?" Before Penny could answer, Chris' forehead wrinkled with a question. "Fire... lady?"

Penny smiled. "No, I'm not, but I am helping your dad with something for the fire department."

"I'm going to be a fireman. When I turn 12, I can join the junior department."

Jacob handed Chris his warm muffin and Penny tapped cinnamon on her frothy drink. Chris worked studiously at the wrapper of the blueberry treat as Penny and Jacob settled into a corner table and took their first sips.

"I asked Roger to meet me here," she said to Jacob in a low voice.

"Why? Are you going to talk to him about Vicki?"

Penny nodded, and Jacob wrinkled his eyebrows in a worried question that mimicked Chris' look a few moments earlier. She held up her hand. "Not that. Paul used his old contacts at the hospital and found out Roger was working a double shift in the emergency room around the time Vicki would have been killed. And it was a busy few days. There was a flu outbreak at the nursing home next to Lazy Pines. His alibi is rock solid."

"So, why are you meeting him? Is it about the Winter Carnival?"

"Yes and no. Arlene asked him to meet me and I'm hoping he'll tell me about some things Vicki might have said in private about the board."

"What's the no part?"

"Mary Barkson told me and Arlene that Vicki was planning on leaving the board. Tammy said she didn't think that was the case but she did say Vicki's been distracted lately. I have a feeling there was something else going on in her life."

"Something? Or someone? Be careful, Penny. That's her husband."

Penny shook her head. "That was Paul's theory, but I don't think there was another man," she said, bringing her voice to a near whisper.

Jacob blew on the rim of his coffee cup while he reached over to Chris to wipe some muffin crumbs from his face.

Roger Truitt entered the Jungle Cafe and the morning din of the busy shop fell to silence as the doctor joined the line of customers waiting for coffee.

He looked freshly showered, his dark hair was still damp and his narrow jaw was clean shaven. He wore a brand of winter parka that Penny knew was pricey and popular in cities like Toronto.

Penny signalled to him and after Roger collected his drink, he approached the corner where she and Jacob waited. Noise returned to the coffee shop as people placed their orders and continued their own conversations, which now likely included talk of the doctor and his dead wife. Penny knew it wasn't just Arlene who wanted answers. Roger and his children didn't have a hope of a normal life in Shells Harbour until Vicki's death was resolved. Roger had a solid alibi, but Penny knew tongues would still wag.

"Thank you for meeting me," Penny said, extending her hand. Jacob did the same and introduced Chris, who had traded his muffin for a video game on his father's phone. Close up, Roger's eyes were red-rimmed, and his skin was sallow. He was clearly exhausted.

"You were both at my wife's memorial," Roger said. "Friends of my sister-in-law, right?"

"That's right," Penny said, and Jacob nodded. "Vicki, too. The girls were so close when we were younger, so if I was spending time with Arlene, I knew Vicki would be there too. She told us the silliest jokes."

Roger's thin lips turned slightly higher at the corners, although Penny wouldn't call his reaction a smile. He took a sip of coffee and Penny realized he hadn't taken off the leather gloves he wore or unzipped his coat. The Shells Harbour winter cold had probably found its way into his bones and taken up residence.

"Can I ask if you have any new information?" Roger looked at Jacob, keeping his voice low. "The police haven't been very helpful."

Jacob shook his head. "I'm waiting on a few test results from inside Coleman's home, but it's slow getting that out of the lab in the city."

Roger slid back into his wooden chair and exhaled in a way that let Penny think he had gotten the answer he was expecting. He turned to her.

"Arlene said you have some questions about the winter carnival," Roger said. "I always supported Vicki. I couldn't make all the meetings because of my work schedule, but I tried to be involved where I could."

"I understand there were some concerns about the finances," Penny said, glancing around the coffee shop to confirm that no one showed signs of listening in.

Roger nodded. "I know Esi's been looking into it. Tammy told me she saw you yesterday. We spoke this morning and she said it looks like someone on the committee was somehow skimming from the finances. Might have even been making up fake invoices, pretending they were a supplier to pay themselves. She doesn't know who, though."

"Do you have any reason to think Vicki might have known what was going on?"

The doctor turned his tired eyes toward Penny, and then looked past her to the Jungle Cafe's bustling parking lot of customers running into the coffee shop with shoulders hunched against the morning cold.

"I'll tell you this, because the police haven't bothered to ask about my wife," he said, without looking away from the window. "Vicki told me this was going to be her last year on the carnival committee. She said she was done with it. I'm ashamed to admit I didn't press her for details. There were a lot of things I should have asked my wife."

When Roger's gaze finally returned to Penny, she saw tears forming in his red eyes. She reached out to cover his hand while Jacob leaned away from the table, as if trying to give Roger more space.

"I don't know how much Vicki knew about the money. I do know she would have had to sign the cheques to make any supplier payments. Whether that means someone figured out how to fake her signature, I just don't know." He exhaled deeply. "My wife was an honest person, and she loved the carnival. I believe she just grew tired of battling with some of the other committee members."

Penny took a quick guess who might have been causing Arlene

problems. Erin Riggings. She nodded to Roger, wanting to end the painful conversation with a grieving man. Penny saw a slight shake in his hands as he pulled the coffee cup to his mouth and took a drink.

"Arlene and I went to see Mary," Penny said. "She told us Vicki had been asking a lot of questions about the family history lately."

"That's true," he said. "She was really interested in her Barkson side. She spent a lot of time with Mary, tracing roots. I should really go see her."

"I think she'd love to see the kids. And you."

That managed to make Roger smile. "Mary Barkson wasn't my biggest fan. Although knowing what this town put Vicki through, I can understand her protectiveness."

"I'd love to know what Vicki might have found out," Penny said.

"You should look at the house. The Barkson house. Vicki was spending time there, looking through some papers and photos." Roger paused and turned to Jacob. "I heard about the fire there, Albert's old truck."

"We think someone was trying to steal it. The truck was far enough away from the house that it didn't spread. Luckily someone driving by saw the smoke."

"That's good then. That place meant a lot to my wife." Roger glanced at the illuminated screen on the face of his watch. "I really should get to work."

He stood up and turned to the door before briefly looking back at Jacob. "Please let me know if you hear anything about the investigation. Someday my kids are going to ask me about this, and I'd like to have answers for them. For all of us."

Jacob agreed. They watched him leave, intercepted briefly by an older couple offering sympathies. He managed to side-step them with a quick, accepting nod.

"Do you believe Roger?" Jacob asked, glancing at Chris to make sure he was still absorbed in his game. "Based on what you know about Vicki and the Winter Carnival, do you really think someone could have been funneling cash right under her nose?"

"I think it's possible, especially if she really was frustrated and ready to quit the committee. And this sudden interest in family history must mean something, doesn't it?"

Jacob sighed. "I don't know. It feels like we're spinning our wheels."

Penny looked around the Jungle Cafe. People leaned into warm mugs and plates of biscuits and muffins. It was always one of the busiest places in Shells Harbour. She thought about the words exchanged across the tables. First dates, business meetings. Old friends catching up. Her eyes settled back on Jacob, who looked up from watching his son play his game.

"I'm just going to say it," Jacob declared. "Sometimes, Penny, I think you might have been right to leave this town."

His words threw Penny. "What do you mean? You love Shells Harbour."

"I do, but this town has a lot of problems," he said. "Someone out there killed Vicki. And we're the ones finding the answers because the cops are too busy handing out parking tickets. Filling up the coffers for town hall."

She leaned into Jacob and kept her voice low. "You and I both know that could happen in any town. Bad things go on everywhere. We're going to find out what happened." Penny surprised herself with a defense of the town, although her optimism wasn't as strong as she pretended it was. "Arlene already asked me to go to the house with her and try to make it look less abandoned, less tempting to the next person who wants to steal something. Maybe we'll see what Vicki found."

Jacob sighed, but Penny could see he was calmer. He took the phone out of Chris' hand, eliciting a grunt of disappointment from the boy. "It's time I drop him off at school and get to the hall."

In truth, Penny was mystified. She'd spent days hoping the carnival committee would unlock answers to Vicki's death, but there was no daylight at the end of that tunnel. Penny knew it was time to dig elsewhere.

Twenty-Two

The old house on Outcrop Road was as orderly as Penny remembered, other than the burned husk of Albert Barkson's truck that sat in a corner of the driveway, waiting for a tow to the junkyard. Dust danced in the air of the kitchen, illuminated by the bright winter sun. Arlene had cracked open a window to let in a gust of cool, fresh air that added even more of a chill to the room. The rooster-themed clock above the dining table was stuck on 4:15 thanks to long-dead batteries. The dishes in the glass-fronted cupboards waited for use that might never come.

There were, though, traces of the most recent occupant of the house. The spectre of the woman who had an affair with Tim lingered, in the pile of dirty clothes left in the washing machine and the smashed family photo that still hung on the wall. Arlene told Penny she made Tim clean up the mess made by the woman who tore a swath of anger through the home, but he had missed a few things.

Penny looked around, feeling the house's haunting by the woman. She thought of the shadow of movement she saw through the window at the truck fire. But Penny now knew Tim's mistress had long since left Shells Harbour and the shadows must have been, as Jacob suggested, just a wisp in her imagination. A memory of a time when the house was warm.

Penny took in the traces of sadness that swirled through the stale air as Arlene tried, without success, to lay a fire in the cold hearth. Penny had already told Arlene about her conversation with Roger, and Vicki's determination to leave the carnival committee this year.

"So, it's just as my grandmother said." Arlene balled up another shred of the newspaper that laid next to the fireplace, probably left by the last tenant. She flicked the lighter she'd pulled out of a kitchen drawer, but the paper had taken in too much of the damp to light. "I was really clueless about what was going on in my sister's life," she said finally. "Do you believe Roger?"

Penny nodded. "I can check with Tammy and Esi to see if they had any hints about Vicki wanting to leave. But I have no reason not to believe Roger. Also, you should know that Paul checked, and he was at work that morning. Vicki had already taken the kids to school, and she might have gone from there to the trailer to meet whoever sent her the message that Jess Anderson saw."

Arlene leaned back on her heels away from the fireplace. "I give up," she said. "I don't know how I'm supposed to make this place look like a home when it hasn't been a real home in years."

Penny helped her friend to her feet and looked around the living room.

"Roger said Vicki was going through documents here, and there might be more she hadn't yet looked at," Penny said. She knew they needed more information to follow on Vicki's trail. "Do you know where they might be?"

Arlene took a deep inhale. "I moved a lot of boxes into the spare room before she rented it out."

Penny didn't need to ask who "she" was. The house's ghost. A woman with a name Penny didn't know, and one that Arlene clearly wouldn't utter.

Albert Barkson had built the house built for his family. It was newer than many in Shells Harbour but the lifelong resident of the town still built it in the style he knew best, like the old captains' houses complete with the widow's perch on the upper floor that faced out toward the roiling Atlantic. The front hallway was narrow and led to the kitchen on the left, where daylight filtered in through fine specks of dust. The lack of human activity took a toll through the winter months.

Arlene stayed silent for a moment. She ran a finger along the edge of the fireplace's mantle and looked up at the wall, to a picture of a youthful Albert and Mary on their wedding day.

"I have nothing but good memories of this place. This was the only house that felt like home to me, even before I actually lived here."

She ran her hand along the flowered wallpaper, her fingers lightly catching the cobwebs that strung across the wall.

"My grandfather changed after Mom got cancer. I didn't see it at the time. I was so sad. But he got angrier. Vicki should have stayed here after mom died, but she went with dad because he was never around and she could do whatever she wanted. Grandpa was torn up by how out-of-control Vicki was. And what it did to my grandmother, trying to get her back on track. They fought about her so much, but I think now it was just because of how sad they were after mom died."

The women slipped from the living room and back into the hallway. Their movements might have seemed aimless, as if they were potential buyers touring an open house. But every inch of the home was dear to Arlene and Penny felt familiarity in the old styling, the wood panelling that was in fashion a few decades ago.

"I'll go get those boxes," Arlene said, mounting the staircase and leaving Penny alone for a few moments.

She touched a divot in the wall and lost herself for a moment in a memory of the first sleepover after Arlene's mother had died. They watched movies and painted their toenails and Penny woke in the night to the sound of Arlene's quiet sobbing, and Mary kneeling next to her granddaughter, stroking her hair.

Arlene came back down the stairs, but she paused and looked up at the sloped popcorn ceiling.

"See that stain there? I shook up a can of pop as hard as I could. It was the first one I ever had. I thought it was like juice and I didn't know you're not supposed to shake it. I think I was about five or six." A smile edged onto Arlene's face and Penny realized it was the first one she'd seen that looked something close to genuine.

"And this orange one next to it. That was Vicki's. We just shook-

shook-shook those cans. When Mary came in, pop dripped from everything. Us, the couch, the carpet."

Arlene's smile turned into laughter at the memory. It started slowly and grew into howls that soon had Penny doubled over as well. Arlene set the box on the floor as their laughter faded. Arlene's tears had turned her eyes glassy and were about to spill down her cheeks. Penny knew she needed to offer the comfort to Arlene that Mary did when they were teenagers. Penny guided her to the sofa and put an arm around her shoulders.

"My sister was murdered. My marriage is over. I'm trying to keep it together for Zach, but I am just sick of it all," Arlene said, wiping at her cheeks. "I'm so tired."

"I know you are," Penny said.

Arlene lifted her head and rubbed her eyes. She surveyed the darkened living room layered in dust. She took a deep breath and then another one, eyebrows knitting together.

"Penny, do you smell that?"

Before Penny could answer, Arlene was out of the living room and grabbing her coat in the kitchen. Penny followed her out of the house and smelled the same thing she had a week earlier in the woods behind Coleridge Coleman's house.

Albert Barkson had built a patio to the left of the house, accessible through the kitchen and it made for the main summertime entrance to the house. Penny and Arlene would lie out on the patio and work on their teenage suntans, flipping through magazines with pop music on Mary's kitchen radio filtering through the screen door.

And now it was in flames. Penny and Arlene plodded through the snow around the house to see a plastic storage container blazing, licking the railing behind it that was covered in a layer of snow but melting fast.

"I'll call the fire department," Penny said. For the second time in as many weeks, she reached into her pocket for her cell phone to call 9-1-1.

Arlene was scooping handfuls of snow to try to put the fire out, but heat from the melting plastic of the container and the yard decorations held inside kept her from getting too close. The winter wind that curled over the road from the ocean was pushing the flames higher and toward the house. Penny described the fire to the dispatcher and gave the address.

Penny was listening to the dispatcher's questions and didn't hear the crunching of the footsteps behind her, but she did catch the wide-eyed look of horror on Arlene's face right before the blow to the back of her head sent her phone flying from her hand and her body tumbling to the snow.

Twenty-Three

Penny felt the cold first, lashing the parts of her skin that were exposed to the snow she laid in. Her hands, her right cheek. Cold. For a moment, that was all she felt.

Until she became aware of sounds. Piercing sirens in the distance grew distinctly closer. From Arlene, she heard her name in a grunted cry. Penny pushed herself up off the snow, digging her icy hands even further into the ground, and felt the blood rush into her throbbing head. Arlene was on her back, struggling to breathe against the knee that an unknown woman was shoving in her gut. The woman had Arlene's hands pinned down at her wrists. Penny hoisted herself off the ground and ran full tilt, driving into the woman in a tackle that knocked her off Arlene.

The woman glared back at Penny. She was pale skinned with blotches of red on her cheeks, like she had been outside for a long time. Her hair was ripped loose from a ponytail and spilled in blond shards around her head. She wore a red puffy winter coat, with the zipper open and underneath, Penny caught sight of a black hooded sweater, edged with blue trim and immediately familiar. It was identical to the one worn by the person who appeared on the trail just after Penny smelled the smoke of Coleridge Coleman's burning home.

"Who the hell are you?" Penny said.

"None of your damn business. My issue ain't with you," the woman said. The cry of the sirens was nearly at the house and almost swallowed her words. "It's with that one."

Arlene was still struggling to catch her breath, but Penny read only confusion in her eyes. She shook her head.

"Oh, she thinks she doesn't know me," the woman said. Her face was burning red now, as bright as the fire that was spreading to the rest of the porch a few feet away and throwing sparks into the evergreens. "You think you don't, but you do. And I will tell you this," she paused, looking up at the firetrucks that were now pulling into the house's dirt driveway, alongside Penny and Arlene's own cars. "We are not done."

The woman fled into the woods. Penny's pounding head gave way to a dizzying nausea and her breakfast threatened to reappear. Arlene's winded lungs barely let her stand up. Neither of them were in any shape to chase after the attacker.

"What the hell is going on?"

Penny heard Jacob's voice before she saw him bounding across the snow toward them. Two firefighters were pulling a hose line through the drifts. Jacob knelt in the snow next to Penny as they opened a stream of water, turning the flames into a sizzling puff of smoke.

"Good lord, you're bleeding," Jacob said. Penny hadn't noticed the blood seeping down the side of her neck until Jacob pointed it out. She hadn't panicked, or screamed, or cried. But the look of fear on Jacob's face made her stomach turn even more, and she clutched his arm. A younger firefighter rushed to them, with a first aid kit in hand, and kneeled next to Jacob, handing him a bandage to cover Penny's wound.

Arlene had already pulled herself to her feet and was squeezing out words.

"That woman. She came out of nowhere."

"Who are you talking about?" Jacob glanced around. The only other woman on the scene was Tammy Johnson, who was on the nozzle of the hose line, drenching the deck.

"She went off into the woods," Penny said, flinching as she held the gauze to the wound on her head. "Ouch. Damn. She came at me from behind. I must have hit a rock or something under the snow when I went down."

Jacob looked into the trees that offered little beyond shadows. The weak winter sun didn't penetrate through bare branches that would, in another few months, spring to life with wide leaves of oak and maple. "Which way did she go?"

Penny glanced at Arlene. They looked for traces of her, but their scuffles had beaten down the snow enough that it was impossible to see where her footsteps might have gone.

"I don't know Jacob. She came out of nowhere and was gone just like that," Penny said. "Arlene, who was she?"

"I have no idea," Arlene replied, her voice wavering.

"Well, she definitely seemed to know you," Penny said, thinking about the woman's open jacket and sweater underneath. She wasn't sure yet whether she should tell Arlene and Jacob about the similarity, but it was hard to imagine there would be two women in Shells Harbour, running through woods in black sweaters, setting fires.

Penny slowly stood up as Arlene stared at the porch, smouldering and dripping with water. Tammy had turned off the nozzle and was also surveying the damage. The firefighters made quick work of the flames that were contained by the layer of snow surrounding the patio. Penny looked at Arlene. It was clear to all of them that things could have been much worse.

"We parked our cars right out front. Whoever that woman is, she set that fire knowing we were inside."

"I'm going to radio for an ambulance," Jacob said, eyeing Penny's wound. "And the police."

"Can you just take me, please? No ambulance. And if you need to call the police, they can talk to me later. They won't catch her now."

Arlene was still silent, looking only at the house, the warped box of yard decorations and the circle of melted snow and soot that stretched out across the deck. Penny saw the tears trickle down Arlene's face. Her head was throbbing, but she shook off Jacob's arm holding her up and crossed to her friend.

"First grandpa's truck, now this," she said. "Whoever that woman was, she has a serious vendetta against my family. She might have killed my sister," Arlene said. "And she could have killed me if you weren't able to tackle her."

"We'll find out who she is," Penny said. "We will."

"Haven't you found out enough? Haven't you found out that this business should be left to the police?" Jacob, Penny, and Arlene hadn't noticed that Deputy Chief Paul Haines had walked past the fire scene over to the beleaguered group. He had arrived in time to hear Arlene's words. "This has all gone far enough," he declared.

They looked at Paul like three teenagers caught spraying graffiti on a school or sneaking home after curfew.

"DC, respectfully, it hasn't. Not when Vicki's killer is still free," Jacob said. "Not when this person is escalating with more fires, and now this attack, if it's the same person."

"They tried to burn down my grandparents' house," Arlene said. "And succeeded in torching my grandfather's truck."

"We can't stop now," Penny said. "Things are coming together. And the police are nowhere to be seen, are they? We're getting close."

Paul shook his head. "Well, I might not convince you to leave the investigation to the professionals, but I can insist that you both go to the hospital and get checked out," he said. "Sheila will have my head if you don't."

Penny tried to smile to reassure Paul she was alright. The women followed the firefighters back through the snowy yard as the others loaded hoses on the truck. But before leaving, Arlene paused and moved back toward the house.

"What are you doing?" Penny called.

"I'm locking the door," she said over her shoulder. "Whoever that was might come back, and I'd like to make it at least a little difficult for them to destroy the place."

Twenty-Four

Penny left the hospital with stitches on her head and orders from Dr. Roger Truitt to avoid electronics until she could be sure the blow hadn't brought a concussion. She opened the door to Sheila's house with relief, feeling the flood of heat from the wood stove and the thick smell of one of her favourite meals, hearty beef stew loaded with meat and vegetables Sheila picked out at the community farmer's market. There would be biscuits from the Jungle Cafe and a pot of warm tea, which would cut through the February chill that settled over Shells Harbour.

Penny slipped out of her snowy boots and hung her coat in the mudroom before stepping into the warmth of the kitchen. She saw they wouldn't be alone for the meal.

"Esi, nice to see you," Penny said, pulling the knit hat off her head and wincing as the fabric brushed tender stitches. Sheila turned from the stove where she was stirring the stew and looked at her niece.

"Paul told me what happened," she said. Penny's stomach sank. Her instinct had been to hide the attack from her aunt, but she knew there'd be no way to do that.

"I feel fine, just a few stitches," Penny said, sliding into a seat at the kitchen table. Sheila scoffed.

"You're not fine," she said. "This is the furthest thing from fine."

Penny moved toward the stove, where Sheila had turned back to the stew pot. She looked at her aunt and saw not anger in Sheila's eyes, but fear. Penny gave Sheila an awkward hug, embracing her side when her aunt refused to turn toward her.

"You're right, I'm not fine," Penny said. "But it's not my head that's the problem. It's that I still don't know what happened to Vicki, and any hope I had of finding out seems to be disappearing. Esi, did you bring more information about the carnival?"

"Yes, but are you sure you're up for it?"

Before Penny could respond, the doorbell chimed. "I invited Arlene for supper. I hope that's alright." She moved toward the entrance. "I didn't want her to be alone, not after today."

"Of course, don't leave her out there in the cold," Sheila said, her words still clipped short.

Penny opened the door for Arlene and ushered her in with a wry smile. "I'm in trouble."

"Yeah, Zach's not too impressed with me, either," Arlene said. "I told him I had an accident, but I think he suspects something else happened. He's hanging out with Jared. I'll pick him up later and get another lecture, I'm sure."

Arlene followed Penny into the kitchen and exchanged greetings with Sheila and Esi. Penny moved to set the dining table, which was only used when guests came for meals.

"I'll help." Arlene carried a stack of plates to the table that she set down with a quiet grunt. "My ribs are pretty sore," she said after Penny raised her eyebrows with concern. "And this isn't pretty," Arlene added, pulling the collar on her shirt to the side to reveal bruises on her shoulder from where the woman held her in the snow.

"I need to tell you something about her," Penny said. "I'm still not sure about this, but when I shoved her off you, I caught a glimpse of a black sweater she was wearing under her coat. And it was only for a few seconds, but the woman I saw running from the fire at Coleridge's trailer was also wearing a black sweater."

Arlene placed a bowl and set cutlery in front of a chair that she pulled out from the table. With a sigh, she sat down.

"That could be something. But I have a black sweater. You were wearing one just the other day. I'm not sure there's a more common piece of clothing in this town during the winter."

She has a point, Penny thought. But it still seemed odd, and more than a coincidence. Arlene looked worn down, defeated, and Penny didn't want to press the issue further.

Sheila carried the pot of simmering stew to the dining table and placed it on a hand-carved trivet. "Everyone, help yourself," she said. After they filled their bowls, Sheila placed the pot on the cast iron wood stove in the adjacent living room, where Smudge was curled up on the couch and lifted his head to sniff the air made enticing by the meal.

Sheila sat at the head of the dining table with Penny at the other end. Esi and Arlene faced each other, and Esi placed a stack of papers next to her. As Penny took in the first mouthfuls of stew, she looked at the files.

"I'd like to know what you've found," Penny said.

"After our meal, please," Sheila said simply. Penny nodded. She respected that she was in Sheila's house, at her table, eating a meal she made. Talk of the carnival could wait.

"Well," Arlene said finally. "I'd like to address another elephant in the room."

The women looked at her, while Arlene took a bite of her biscuit drenched in stew. "This is delicious, by the way. Thank you for having me, Sheila."

"My pleasure. But what's the elephant?"

"It's been what, two, three months since you've been home, Penny? Forgetting the fact that you didn't bother to visit me until my sister died, I still would love to know what brought you back to our little berg after all those years away?"

Penny gulped down her food and wiped her mouth with a napkin. Sheila had never asked, although Penny knew she was curious. Blunt Arlene would be the only one to bring it up, and only in her unique way.

"Come on, spill. I think we can all agree I'm having a pretty awful week," Arlene said. "I'd like to think about something else."

"Okay, okay," Penny relented. "It's not much of a story, though."

Penny told Arlene, Sheila and Esi about how her relationship had unravelled, leaving out the worst of the details of Callum's infidelity and lies, but offering enough to let them know the relationship was untenable.

"There was always something off about that Callum," Sheila said, shaking her head. "I knew he wasn't right for you. Remember when I came to visit for Easter last year? I just wanted to treat the two of you to a nice dinner. And he acted like I was accusing him of being cheap. Like I was saying he couldn't afford to give us a night out."

Penny nodded. "When I started putting some pieces together, I realized that was around the time he had started seeing the woman he met online."

"How did you find out?" Esi asked, leaning forward with attention.

"You know, I don't post a lot on social media. But I put up a few pictures after Callum and I went to Banff last summer. I tagged him so it showed up on his timeline. And I think that's what made her contact me. He had lied to her and told her he was single. She sent me plenty of evidence. I had no doubt she was telling the truth." Penny knew she was speaking matter-of-factly, as if she was talking about a long day at work or a bout with the flu. "After everything shook out, Toronto just didn't feel the same. My desk job was swallowing me up. I wanted to work with writers and develop books and that wasn't happening. So, I came home to lick my wounds."

"Do you think you'll go back to Toronto?" Arlene asked. Penny shook her head.

"There's nothing for me there."

"I don't know if there's a good way to find out that your partner is being unfaithful, but at least you got to make a clean break," Arlene said. "I don't get that with Tim."

Penny looked at her friend, who had her head down and was scooping up another mouthful of stew. Sheila got up from the table to bring the pot from the stove for seconds.

"No, I suppose you don't," Penny said. "How is Zach handling things?"

"As best as he can. He's with me most of the time until Tim finds a permanent home, and we'll sort out custody. Zach doesn't enjoy being at the Lighthouse Motel with his dad. He calls it the sad men's hotel," Arlene said. That elicited a chuckle from the other women.

"Tim is following a not-so-proud Shells Harbour tradition of getting kicked out of the house for drinking or cheating or, sad to say, beating," Sheila said.

"I only have one of those three," Arlene said. "Although Tim did try to claim he only slept with Deana when he was drunk. As if that excuses his behaviour."

"No, it certainly does not," Esi said. The women fell silent as they finished the last bites of their meal and Sheila left the kitchen to put the kettle on for tea. Penny settled into the warmth of the house and the conversation. Even though they were talking about the breakups of relationships, it still soothed her to be at a table with family and friends, rather than in her cold apartment in the city, alone.

Esi paused for a moment before her eyes turned to the papers she'd placed on the table between them. "What did you say her name is, Arlene?"

"Who?"

"Tim's mistress."

"Oh. Deana something. Sampson, maybe? I don't know much about her. I don't think she's from around here. She definitely would have known Tim was a married man. Half of his office knew me."

With the meal over, Esi thumbed through the documents she had put on the table. Penny recognized them as budget papers, the Winter Carnival documents Esi had been delving into before Vicki was killed. Sheila poured milk as Esi pulled one document from her stack.

"Here," she said, sliding it onto the chestnut brown table toward Penny, while Arlene moved her chair closer.

The paper was a letter, signed by an accounting firm with an address in the city. "It's an audit report," Penny said. "It says they have confirmed the financial results as accurate."

"Look who signed it."

Underneath the letter affirming that the report was accurate, a name was printed, and a signature scrawled beneath. Deana Simpson.

Twenty-Five

Penny slept fitfully, waking up with a need for coffee and a hot shower to wash off the weight that had sunk over her. The stitches in her head were sore, but she gently lathered her brown hair around it, wincing as she bundled it in a towel a little too tightly.

The kitchen already smelled like coffee when Penny emerged from the shower and Sheila was stirring a pot of burbling oatmeal at the stove.

"How late were you up last night?" Sheila asked Penny as she poured a cup.

"Just a little after midnight. I wanted to see for myself what Esi said about the carnival's finances."

"And? Did you confirm it? Does it make sense?"

Penny took a sip of her coffee and looked at her aunt with raised eyebrows.

"Since when are you interested in this?"

Sheila turned toward Penny and immediately, she could tell her aunt probably hadn't slept much, either. Penny felt another stab of regret that she was causing her to worry.

"Clearly you and Arlene need some adult supervision, so take me through what you found out."

Penny swallowed her surprise along with another gulp of coffee and looked at the files Esi had left on the kitchen table after dinner, as Sheila ladled out two bowls of steaming cinnamon raisin oatmeal and sprinkled them with brown sugar.

"Well, we know the woman Tim had an affair with is the same as the woman who was approving the audits of the winter carnival. And we know the carnival was losing money somewhere. Esi said the committee's policy was always to buy local."

Penny pulled a budget statement from the papers and looked at the column of numbers. "Look at this one. They agreed to buy new cloth table coverings to decorate the community centre for the carnival ball. This was last year. The invoice is for $2,000," Penny said. "So that's what the committee should have paid to the supplier."

"That's one that Esi checked, right?"

Penny nodded. "Swishes was listed as the supplier, so she checked with Jess Anderson. But Jess said the contract for tablecloths was half the invoiced amount. Only $1,000."

"What do you think it means?"

"That someone has been overcharging the committee and issuing fake invoices from real suppliers," Penny said. "Esi said the numbers don't make sense, but she won't be able to check them all the same way she did for the Swishes contract. There are too many."

The papers were columns of text and numbers. Revenue, donations, fees, expenses. Penny knew Sheila would have an idea what she was looking at, from years as a small business owner when she'd hand over her receipts every spring to her accountant.

Penny could see how easily the numbers could be passed off as accurate. They all looked official, and they had verification from auditors. Deana Simpson had only signed off on the papers for the last two years and had approved both within recent months. Before then, the committee used a different auditing company, a name Penny recognized as a local firm.

"Here's when they switched from Harbour Accounting to the city firm."

"Esi said switching was Vicki's idea too, another attempt to save money. Sail Away uses that firm from the city, Deana's company."

"Sail Away?" Penny asked. She wasn't sure if her memory was foggy from the lack of sleep or the blow to the head. "I don't remember us talking about this last night."

"We didn't talk about it very much over dinner. But Esi was upset about it when they made the change. Sail Away is Erin's husband's shop. He took early retirement from Prime Ocean and opened it to make custom sails for fancy boats."

Penny nodded slowly.

"Everyone said Vicki wanted to save the carnival money. That's why she made them get quotes from outside the area. Although it looks like they almost always went with the local option, apart from the auditor," Penny said.

"I wonder why Deana Simpson was signing off on these audits," Sheila said. "If Vicki was stealing money, why would the woman who was sleeping with her sister's husband help her hide it?"

"You think she knew?"

"She would have had to," Sheila said. "Deana was either extremely negligent in her audit, or she was in on it. These expenses make no sense."

The doorbell, a melodic wind chime sound, echoed in the front hall and Penny pushed back away from the table to answer the door. She moved a little too quickly and tried to hide the rush that came to her head, but her grip on the table gave her away. Sheila looked at her with concern.

"It's okay," Penny said as loosened her grip on the table.

"There's nothing okay about this," Sheila said, speaking to Penny as much as to the papers on the table.

Jacob Bell waited on the doorstep with Chris. The child had wrapped his mittened hands around a small potted cactus. When Penny opened the door, the two looked at her with identical faces of concern and Chris reached out with the plant.

"I told him you had an accident, and he was worried," Jacob said.

"We got this for you. I don't know what it is, I picked it out and it's got prickles," Chris said. "Dad said you'd like it."

"Well, he was right," Penny said with a wide smile. She took the pot from the boy and stepped back to let them in from what was turning out to be a chilly winter day.

Jacob and Chris followed Penny into the kitchen and Jacob accepted the cup of coffee Sheila offered. Chris took a glass of apple juice.

"Can I see your stitches?" Chris asked Penny without a trace of the shyness he had at their first meeting. Penny laughed and leaned over so he could see the healing cut on her head. Chris looked and leaned back, satisfied, and sipped his juice.

"I'm sorry I couldn't stay with you at the hospital. Chris was sick at school and I had to go pick him up," Jacob said.

"I barfed!"

Penny and Sheila laughed.

"Yeah, all over the gym floor," Jacob said, grimacing. "Mr. Nickerson was not pleased and called Chris' mom. She was busy with a client, so I went to pick him up and kept him out of school today."

"Just in case I barf again," Chris said.

"Mr. Nickerson," Penny said. "Remember how he would make us race those scooters across the gym floor? It always ended in carnage. A pile of kids in tears and bruises."

Chris guffawed at the image and Jacob rushed to grab his apple juice before he knocked it over, which made the boy laugh even harder. Penny was glad for levity that took her mind off the pile of papers on the kitchen table.

When they calmed down, Penny explained to Jacob what Esi had shared the night before. She dropped child-friendly hints to him about Deana and her relationship with Arlene's husband. Penny could see that he was as puzzled about the connections as she and Sheila were.

Sheila placed her empty oatmeal bowl in the sink and gathered her purse and tote bag to ready herself for work.

"Take care of this one, Jacob," Sheila said, nodding toward Penny. He nodded, a little more seriously than she would have liked. After Sheila left, she poured Chris another cup of apple juice and coffee for her and Jacob.

"The more we find out, the less it all makes sense to me," Penny said, exhaling deeply. "How do you do it? Investigate fires?"

"That's just it though," Jacob said. "I investigate fires. Not people. Fires make a lot more sense than people."

Penny thought about that as she sipped from her warm mug. She knew nothing about fire investigation, but presumably there was a science to it. To how fires burned and consumed whatever they could.

But then, people were like that too, Penny thought. Some people. They ate up what they could of others, leaving charred remains behind. That's what the last year of her relationship with Callum was like. And maybe that's what Arlene's marriage was like. A burned shell of what once was. Penny thought about Callum's betrayal, and that made her return to Deana.

"Arlene said Deana was renting her grandparents' house when she was in town, working with Tim at Prime Ocean," Penny said. "Tammy doesn't think Vicki was involved in the committee's financial issues. But then again, she doesn't know about Deana Simpson's connection to it all. Esi just connected those dots last night."

"Maybe there's more information in the house," Jacob said. "More papers there?"

"We were going to look at some yesterday, before the fire. I'd like to go back and find them," Penny said. "If Arlene agrees, are you two up for a little adventure?"

"Yeah!" Chris said. "As long as I don't barf again."

Jacob looked at both of them and groaned, which Penny took as agreement. She sent a quick text message to Arlene, asking her to meet them before grabbing her coat, scarf, hat, and gloves. Her head felt woozy and full for a moment and she looked at Jacob, who had noticed her wobble. She forced a smile.

"You drive."

Twenty-Six

"Can I get a muffin, Dad? Please?"

Jacob turned to look at his son in the back seat. The boy's skin was still pale, but the dark circles that rimmed his eyes had brightened.

"How about a little toast and some juice? Let's see how your tummy handles that. Coffee?" Jacob directed the last part at Penny, who was in the front seat of his truck. She nodded, distracted, staying silent until the hot paper cup was in her gloved hands. She was polite enough to remember to thank him, but her anxiety mounted as they left the coffee shop drive through and headed toward Outcrop Road.

"How does your head feel?" Jacob asked Penny. Chris was devouring his toast with a noisy dedication in the back seat.

Penny reached a hand to her stitches. "It's okay. A little sore."

"Any more dizziness?"

Penny shook her head lightly. Jacob brought his truck into the freshly plowed driveway. Arlene had arranged for the clearing in her effort to maintain the house and make it look occupied. The winter sun shone off the windows, offering no hint of what might be inside the darkened interior.

Across Outcrop Road, the waves churned, even though the weather conditions were still. In a storm, the ocean would be brutal. The wind would be as sharp as a rider's crop, with ice and sleet that pelted hard, lashing exposed skin. Winters along the coast were harsh, but so were the summer rains and fall tropical storms. To live a lifetime along the Atlantic meant battening down the hatches, time and again.

Penny pulled herself out of the truck and glanced up at the shutters, swung closed on the upper floor to protect the windows from storms. Before the attack, Penny and Arlene hadn't been able to make the house look lived in as a deterrent to vandals and thieves. And even though Arlene told Mary she would hold off on deciding about selling the house, Penny hoped her friend could come to a resolution about letting it go and taking at least one burden off her shoulders.

Arlene's SUV pulled in behind Jacob's truck. She wore a long black coat and a matching purple knit hat and scarf, a colour that had the effect of making her pale skin look almost translucent. Penny handed her a cup of coffee they'd picked up for her.

"I need to tell you both something," Arlene said, as she sipped the hot drink. "After Tim's affair, I avoided looking up his mistress on social media. I didn't want her in my head any more than she was. But after what we found out last night about the audit, I did it."

Penny glanced at Jacob. Chris was playing in the snow.

"It's her, Penny. The woman who set the fire and attacked us. Right here." Arlene looked at the charred deck.

"But why?" Penny asked. "You and Tim are separated. Why come after you now?"

Arlene could only shake her head and she turned to slide her key into the door's lock. Chris had busied himself rolling a ball of snow and asked if he could keep playing outside while the adults went into the house.

"I can't even think of when the last time there would have been a snowman in this yard," Arlene said, pulling the hat from her head as she stepped over the threshold. She paused and looked back at Jacob. "You should tell him to yell if anyone approaches him. Tim's mistress could be hiding anywhere."

Jacob considered this for a moment. He turned back to Chris. "Buddy, come inside for now. We'll finish your snowman later."

Chris groaned and thudded up the steps toward the front door. He crossed through the doorway, then paused and looked ahead into the dim mid-morning light that brought only limited visibility into the room. "Wait, whose house is this?"

"It's my grandmother's," Arlene told him simply, leaving out the layers of tangles and connections the house had wrought. For Chris, that was enough.

"Cool. Can I look around?"

"You can look with your eyes but not your hands, okay?" Jacob said and Chris was gone into the darker recesses of the house, his youthful bravery and curiosity propelling him forward. Penny knew the house was structurally sound and the biggest problem Chris would encounter would be the layer of dust that had settled over the furniture since Deana Simpson moved out.

Arlene turned left into the kitchen and opened the door that led to the deck Deana had set ablaze. The charring had been contained to the box of summer supplies she'd used as a fire starter, but they knew it was only the coating of snow that kept the fire from spreading. The heat from the flames had bubbled the paint from the side of the house.

"I'm still unsure whether she started the fire hoping it would spread quickly and trap us inside, or if her plan was exactly what happened. Lure us outside and attack," Arlene said.

"Possibly both," Jacob said. "When the fire didn't spread, and you came outside, she might have decided to take her chance. I just don't know why she thought two against one was a good idea."

"She must be desperate, although I can't imagine why," Arlene said. "And she didn't know that Penny played rugby in high school."

Penny heard this conversation from across the hallway. She had turned right into the living room rather than left with Arlene and Jacob. She found the banker's box Arlene had placed on the floor when they rushed outside toward the fire.

Residual heat flowed into the room after Penny opened the curtains, cutting the winter chill. She had plenty of daylight now to see the papers piled high inside the box when she lifted the lid off.

"Arlene, do you know what's in here?"

Jacob and Arlene crossed into the living room. Arlene looked inside, and Penny saw thin wrinkles pinched on her forehead.

"My grandmother boxed up a lot of papers before she moved into Lazy Pines, and we put them in the spare room when that woman moved in. That was just the first one I could grab, although it was sitting on top with the lid half off. It made me think Vicki had looked through it.

Penny nodded. "Roger said Vicki was interested in some documents here. Part of her digging into the family past."

Arlene kneeled next to Penny. "Well, if that's the case, let's see what she might have found."

On top was the deed and title registration that described the swath of Albert Barkson's property, the house, and the land that caused a rift between Arlene and Vicki.

"It's strange that Vicki would just leave these here. These are important papers," Arlene said. "Although maybe she planned to come back for them."

Penny paused as the implication of Arlene's words settled over them. Vicki would never be coming back. "I don't know if there's anything in here that can help us figure out what might have gotten Vicki in trouble," Penny said. "But if there's even a chance that Deana would come back here and cause more problems, we need to have time to look through them ourselves."

"You're right. And now I'm wondering whether she tried to steal my grandfather's truck, too," Arlene said. "I wish I had convinced Gram just to get rid of it. It's too old for Zach to drive when he turns 16."

"Is that why she was keeping it around?"

Arlene nodded. "She thought it was something the boys could share. Zach and Jared."

Jacob joined them on the faded burgundy and beige oriental rug as they pulled out papers. Penny flipped through an old bank book where someone had recorded deposits and withdrawals in tidy ink. She looked at the date on the cover, 1974. The inside pages showed deposits from a business called Fancy Point Processing.

"What's Fancy Point?" Penny asked the others. Arlene shook her head, but Jacob thought for a moment.

"I think that's an old canning factory. Out in the Valley."

"A canning factory?"

"Yeah, they put produce in cans and shipped them to grocery stores around the province. Tomatoes and beans and the stuff that the farmers grew out there. It's all done by big factories out of the province now. I'd bet that place is long closed," Jacob said. He looked at the numbers. "Did one of your grandparents work there, Arlene?"

"I don't know," she said, taking the bank book from Penny and turning it over in her hands. "My grandmother was a nurse and my grandfather worked with Werston's Construction. These deposits look regular. They must have been paycheques."

The neat handwriting showed deposits from another source. Consistently, month after month, a deposit of $25 from M.B., and the cheque number.

"Look at this," Penny said, showing them the bank book, the listing of deposits. "M.B. Could be Mary Barkson, right?"

"It could be. Is it my grandfather's? Maybe he worked at the cannery for a while and Mary had to give him money for some reason," Arlene said. Penny looked at the inside cover of the deposit book.

"Annette Ross. Who's that?"

"Never heard of her," Jacob said. Arlene shook her head.

At a creak in the floorboard, Penny looked up. She sprung off the cold wooden floor, tripping over the lid of the box as she did and stumbling backward. Before Jacob or Arlene could move to help her, a voice from behind froze them.

"That's my mother. You should have heard of her. Everyone in this damn town should know her name."

Twenty-Seven

Coleridge Coleman emerged from the shadow of a dark hallway that opened onto the southern end of the living room. He looked as if he had been living in a hole. His jacket hung limply from his shoulders. His grey hair was stringy, and his cheeks were hollow. Penny realized he must have been hiding out in the house, possibly for days, since the fire at his own home. Even when she and Arlene were attacked outside.

And now he had a grip on Jacob's young son, Chris.

Arlene gasped. Jacob lunged forward to grab the boy, and Penny, her head throbbing, moved out of his way. Jacob swooped at Coleman before any of them saw the buck knife in his right hand, tucked behind his back. He dropped his grip on Chris and slashed the blade toward Jacob.

Penny grabbed the boy and pushed him toward Arlene, who was already tapping 9-1-1 on her phone's screen. Arlene held Chris tightly while Penny saw blood ooze from Jacob's arm.

"Dad!" Chris cried from behind Arlene. She pulled the boy into the hallway while reciting the Outcrop Road address for the operator.

Penny looked around the sparse living room for anything that she could use as a weapon while Coleridge circled a bleeding Jacob. Coleridge's eyes were bulging, and Penny thought she saw fear in them. Still, if he was thinking about making another swipe, she needed to act.

"Coleridge, stop!" Arlene called. "Put the knife down." But she couldn't sway him. Penny remembered that one of Mary Barkson's heavy wooden rolling pins hung on a wall in the kitchen, a relic from a time when the house seemed warm and happy, full of smells like burbling chicken stew and baking bread. Penny had no time to wonder about the real secrets held in the happy home as she made a quick dash, sliding the dusty pin off the wall.

The living room had two entrances along the hallway and Penny used the further one, the same way Coleridge used to make his sudden appearance with Chris. She needed to catch him off guard.

"Shoulda just left me alone," Coleridge growled at Jacob, who was holding his wounded arm while trying to create distance between them. "I was alright there, never needed to be found. None of this needed to happen."

The cut on Jacob's arm weakened him, so Penny quickly realized it was up to her to stop the angry older man. Penny took her chance, swinging the rolling pin into Coleridge's side to cripple him with a blow to a kidney.

Coleridge slumped to his knees and clutched his middle. Penny scooped to pick up the knife that had slipped from his hand. She tossed it on the couch and rushed to Jacob as Coleridge gasped.

"I'm okay, I'm okay," Jacob said, bleeding heavier now from his wound. Penny knew she needed to move quickly for Jacob, but Coleridge had to be secured. "Get that rope." Jacob pointed to a decorative tie holding back one of Mary's sheer grey curtains. Penny snatched it off the hook.

"Roll him over and sit on him," Jacob instructed. Penny grabbed the still gasping Coleridge by his arm and flipped him onto his stomach. His lightness surprised her, given his fight with Jacob. He had been living rough, that was clear, and he seemed to have no struggle left in him when Penny held his hands behind his back.

"Stupid, stupid, stupid," Coleridge muttered, his words breathless and tired. They seemed to be directed at himself rather than anyone in the room. "Shoulda just left me alone."

Jacob moved to them and drew loops around the man's wrists. "Pull here, Penny," he told her, and she saw he didn't have enough strength in his arm to tug the rope taut. "Handcuff knot. We use it to rescue victims, but it has other purposes."

Penny climbed off Coleridge's back and left him on the floor. Arlene pressed a dish towel into Jacob's wounded arm while Chris huddled in the doorway, eyes wide and filled with tears.

"I'm okay buddy, don't worry, just a few scratches."

"I'm sorry Dad, I found his hiding spot, and he showed me the knife and told me not to scream," Chris said, his voice wavering. Jacob took the towel from Arlene and pressed to his arm by himself so he could kneel in front of his son.

"You did the right thing, Chris. Listen to me. You brought him right to us and we're all safe now."

Chris sniffed and nodded his head as the sound of sirens grew louder. Arlene kneeled next to Coleridge, and Penny could see her old friend's eyes were burning red.

"Are you living here? Are you squatting in this house? My grandparents' house?"

He rolled his head to the other side, but that didn't stop Arlene. He was powerless and prone. Arlene motioned for Penny to help her, and they pulled the man up by his armpits and sat him on the couch, hands still tied. Penny picked up the knife she had tossed on the couch and held it in her hand. Coleridge was bound, but she couldn't be sure how durable Jacob's knot was and she didn't want to risk him getting his hands on the weapon again.

"Did you kill my sister?" Arlene demanded a response from the subdued man. "Did you kill Vicki? Why was she in your trailer?"

Coleridge looked at Arlene and blinked, his wrinkled eyes nearly hidden by his overgrown, greying hair.

"Give me an answer, dammit!"

The front door burst open, thudding against the inner wall with a bang. Constable Wally McPhee burst into the room with all the energy of a cop in a quiet town who'd been dispatched to a proper emergency.

"Everyone stop," he yelled. Chris huddled behind his father's legs. Arlene and Penny froze where they were near Coleridge on the couch.

Wally had his hand on the holster of his handgun and looked rapidly between Jacob and Chris to Coleridge, Penny and Arlene. Jacob held his one hand at chest height, keeping the other on the towel and the wound.

"It's okay, McPhee, we're under control," the fire captain said. Penny understood why the police and firefighters would know each other in a small town like Shells Harbour, where their calls for service would certainly overlap often. "I wouldn't mind getting to the hospital though, if I could."

Wally McPhee looked at Jacob and then Penny, who was still holding the knife.

"Ma'am, put that knife down now," the officer said sharply, his fingers twitching on the gun still in its holster. "On the floor. Right now."

"Okay, okay," Penny said, feeling heat rush into her cheeks. She put the knife on the ground and pushed it away with her foot. Wally moved toward her and retrieved it. He nodded toward Coleridge. "Why's this one tied up?"

"I ain't saying nothing. To any of you," Coleridge replied, looking at Arlene first and then at the officer.

Penny gave Wally a quick version of the events. Her retelling, and Jacob's wound, were sufficient evidence for the police officer to tug Coleridge off the sofa and replace the curtain tie with proper handcuffs.

In the cool air of the late winter morning, Wally placed Coleridge Coleman in the back of his cruiser.

"I'll need statements from you all later," he said, opening the door to the driver's seat.

"You're the officer I chatted with last week, aren't you? The one from Cape Breton," Penny asked. Wally nodded, his brown eyes narrowing.

"You're dating the deputy mayor's daughter."

He cleared his throat. "I am. Why?"

"Oh, I've just been trying to figure out why the Shells Harbour police officer who's dating Lowell Cranson's daughter seems to have been following me around town for the past week."

Jacob and Arlene, who had been locking up the house, looked up at this.

"He's been doing what?" Jacob asked, his voice rising enough to catch Chris' attention. The boy had calmed down and was back at work on his abandoned snowman.

"I haven't been following you around," Wally said. "You happen to be doing my job."

"What are you talking about?"

"Mrs. Truitt was murdered. I'm a police officer," he said, exasperation in his voice. "The police are supposed to investigate murders, not civilians like you."

"You're a constable," Arlene said. "I thought Detective Sutton was investigating my sister's death."

Wally McPhee's scoff was fast and his boyish, round cheeks reddened. Penny guessed he was probably teased about that a lot in his youth, possibly still was on the police force.

"Pardon my French, but Sutton couldn't detect a frog in a pond," he said, prompting a giggle from Chris. "Thought if I could bring in something extra, the chief would put me on the case too. Maybe make me a detective. And now I have my chance, thanks to you folks, who have delivered me Coleridge Coleman on a platter."

Wally slid into the cruiser and pulled out of the driveway, the bar of lights still flashing on top of the car. They looked after him for a moment.

"Why do I feel like any chance I had of finding out what happened to my sister is slipping down that road?"

Penny moved to Arlene's side.

"We're far from done. We're going to figure this out. Did you get those papers?"

Arlene nodded. "The box is in the backseat of my car. Coleridge said they were his but if he's squatting in my grandparents' house, he has no right to them."

"Perfect. I'm going to get this one stitched up, get this one a muffin, and get some coffee for us so we can keep going through those documents," she said, looking first to Jacob and then Chris, who had broken into a smile at the mention of a muffin.

"Get a blueberry scone if you're going to Jungle Cafe. My grandmother loves them, and I think we owe her another visit."

Twenty-Eight

Mary Barkson looked at the papers her granddaughter had laid out before her. Her eyes were bright and clear. She'd pushed aside the half-eaten blueberry scone. With every document, Mary offered a slight nod, as if she had been expecting this to come.

"So, this is why Vicki developed her interest in family history," Mary said, gently leaning back in her chair. "You found these papers in the house? And you think Coleridge was squatting there?"

Arlene nodded. Penny stood apart from the women, leaning near the sink. She wanted to be present, but also allow them their moment.

"Vicki must have been digging for a long time to come up with all this," she said, her voice cracking slightly at the mention of her other granddaughter. "Although, these aren't my bank records, are they? These have Annette's name on it."

"You knew her?"

Mary looked up from the table.

"I did. A long time ago. I hoped I'd never hear tell of her again," she said. "But there are some things that you can't escape from. And things I should have told you before. Penny, put the kettle on, please. I need some more tea."

A quiet settled over the women as the water burbled in the electric kettle and Penny poured it into a ceramic pot. Penny could tell Arlene was itching for more answers, while Mary seemed to prepare herself to open an old wound that had never fully healed. She looked every inch the role of a grandmother in her 80s, with her orthopedic shoes and embroidered sweater. Brown age spots marked her wrinkled hands. She poured a dollop of milk in her mug and blew across the surface of her tea.

"There are people in this world, they want for nothing. But they don't see it, so they want everything. Bertie was like that. Vicki must have got it from him," Mary said. "It was that wanting that got her married to that doctor fellow. Nice enough, but he's grey like dishwater. Not the type to keep Vicki happy. And she knew it. She was ready to up and leave those little ones with Roger. She wanted out of Shells Harbour."

"What are you talking about, Grandma?" Arlene asked. "I had no idea about this."

"Secrets and lies. Vicki had them both in spades," Mary said. "A few months back, she came to me. She wanted me to write over the title for the house and the land to her so she could sell it. She said she had some developer interested in it and Albert's dream would finally be realized."

"He did always want to do something with the land," Penny said, playing a cautious devil's advocate.

"Vicki didn't care about any wish of her grandfather's. She wanted to sell the land, take the money and leave her husband and children. She's always hated this town, and she got married way too young. I told her she should talk to her husband about it, but she just wanted to leave. I said if she wanted to do that, she'd have to get agreement in writing from the other heirs to the property. The people who will get it when I'm gone."

"I didn't know she was so unhappy in her marriage. In her life," Arlene said. "Vicki had been talking about the land a lot over the past few months, but she said nothing to me about selling it."

"I'm not talking about you, my girl," Mary said. "I figured Vicki would wear you down eventually, especially given everything going on with your husband."

"You think my sister would have taken advantage of my divorce to convince me to sign off on a land sale?"

"I know it. You're better now, but when Tim was doing his nonsense, running around with that woman, you weren't yourself," Mary said. Penny stayed silent, feeling again a stab of pain for her friend.

"You're right, of course," Arlene said, taking a long sip of her own tea. "I just can't believe Vicki would leave her family. Her children. I know she wasn't happy about some things and Becky had been acting up a lot." She stopped, shaking her head. "But what does that have to do with all these old records?"

"Well, like I said, I told Vicki that she'd have to get approval from all of Albert's heirs. You girls, who hold your mother's share. And the share for his son."

"His what?"

Arlene sat back in her chair quickly, sending her teacup clattering to the floor as she knocked into the table. Penny rushed to the kitchen sink for paper towels to sop up the brown mess that spread along the floor.

"Oh, the papers," Arlene cried, grabbing more towels.

"It's okay, it's okay," Mary said, grabbing her granddaughter's frantic hand. "You barely touched them. Penny, how's my floor looking?"

Penny stood up from her squat with a bundle of tea-soaked paper towels. "Perfectly fine, Mary," she said.

"Good. That's about the same reaction your sister had, by the way, only I think it was a glass of juice. Yes indeed, I ruined all her fine plans."

Arlene pushed away from the table and stood, taking a long moment to steady herself. Mary's apartment was small and styled in an open flow from the kitchen into the living room. Arlene crossed the space and stood in front of a picture window, looking toward the Lazy Pines parking lot and beyond, where white caps on the ocean roiled.

"You and grandpa had a son?"

"No, not me and your grandfather. Albert had a child with her," she said, tapping the papers on the table. "Annette Ross. My husband had an affair. A little boy was born out of it."

"Oh no, Mary," Penny said softly, reaching for her hand. Arlene was still looking out the window at the greying sky. "That's Coleridge, isn't it? When he confronted us at the house, he said Annette was his mother, and we should all know it." Penny flashed to the moment with a terrified Chris, a bleeding Jacob, and the thud of connecting Mary's rolling pin with Coleridge's body.

"Albert swore the child wasn't his," Mary said. "The woman was a troublemaker, he said. A liar. She was the secretary at the farm where he went to work one summer over in the valley, one year when things were real tight and there wasn't much work paving the roads or nothing. The fish plant wasn't taking anyone extra on. There was almost no work around here. He went picking vegetables and delivering them to the cannery out there. Annette worked in the office. The next spring, she showed up with a little one."

Arlene had wandered back to the table and stared down at her hands, folded in her lap. Penny looked between grandmother and granddaughter. Mary's pain resonated with her every word, and Penny knew Arlene felt it deeply. The wounds of cheating spouses had cut both of them to pieces.

"She came to the house?" Arlene finally said, gently urging her grandmother on. Mary nodded.

"Like I said, Bertie said the little one wasn't his, but I knew it the moment that girl knocked on my door. The baby had Bertie's eyes, his nose, the same one I saw on your mother's face when she was born. I told the girl if she'd shut up about it, we'd square her away. There'd be something in her bank account every month till that boy turned 16."

"Did you ever hear from her again?"

"Never. She took that money and ran. At some point I thought if she came back and told all it'd be alright, but she never did," Mary said. "I set it up with my cousin at the bank that they'd take out the money every month, so in time I nearly forgot about it. Was never the same between me and Bert, but I wasn't about to hand the life I'd worked for over to another woman."

"Grandma, I'm so sorry," Arlene said. "I just can't imagine how painful that had to have been for you. I can't believe Grandpa did that."

"He mellowed out a lot by the time you girls came along. He was a different man in his old age, at least until your mother died. But I think he wished he knew what happened to the baby. When Vicki came to me about the land, with nothing but greed in her eyes, I wanted to take her down a peg. Guess I've always been trying to take that girl down a few, since she was a teenager. And see where it got her."

Tears gathered in Mary's eyes. Arlene moved out of her chair and stood over the woman before leaning low and holding her tightly. Mary Barkson, a strong woman stooped by time and secrets, stiffened for a moment before allowing her last granddaughter to comfort her.

"I wish Vicki could have just been happy," Mary said, between sobs. "She should have just let it all go."

After they'd settled, and Mary had dabbed her eyes with a tissue, Penny spoke.

"Vicki didn't though, did she? She didn't let any of it go."

Mary looked at Penny and Arlene.

"Not for a single second," Mary said. "But that was my fault. I told Vicki she had to find everyone else entitled to a share of that land. That may not have been the law, but that was my say. She had to find Bertie's son before I'd sign off on anything. As his wife, that house and land are mine to decide on. She didn't like that, but off she went to track him down."

"And she found him. Right here in Shells Harbour."

Mary moved her hand to her face and nodded slowly. "From what you've told me, there must be so much anger inside that man for everything that happened. This is my fault. I should have just let Vicki do what she wanted with that house. Her digging brought him into her life and it probably got her killed."

Penny mulled that thought over while Mary shook, tears in her eyes. It didn't make sense that Coleridge would kill Vicki, but then leave Arlene alone. He'd had the opportunity to attack her at the house but didn't do anything beyond his awkward slash at Jacob. And he barely struggled when Penny bound his hands with the curtain ties. Vicki was young, and healthy. It's hard to think that she wouldn't have been able to fight off Coleridge, who was rail-thin and had a bad leg.

"How did Vicki find him?" Arlene asked when Mary calmed.

Mary let her hand slide into her lap. "The damn computer, of all things. I didn't really follow what she was telling me, but she said something about a computer group for lost relatives. She put Annette's name out to the group and got a response from someone saying that was her grandmother."

"Grandmother? Does Coleridge have children?" Penny looked at Arlene, who shrugged.

"I know nothing about him. He appeared in town maybe 20 years ago. Started working at the mill and he didn't go far. Bought that piece of land next door and put his trailer on it."

"Did Vicki say if she ever met the woman who claimed to be Annette's granddaughter? And why would Annette's banking records be there, in your house?"

Mary looked down at the table and shook her head. "She was going to come back last week and tell me more. Obviously, she didn't make it."

Twenty-Nine

Penny emerged from the warm interior of Lazy Pines into the greyness of the winter afternoon and looked up at the sky.

"Looks like at least one more storm before we finally get to spring," she said to Arlene, who was red-eyed and still shaking her head in disbelief about what her grandmother had revealed.

"Secrets always come out, don't they? I could have made it through my whole life without knowing who my grandfather really was."

"Albert Barkson loved you, Leenie. That was clear to anyone who saw him dote on you and Vicki."

"But to put my grandmother through that," Arlene said. "Imagine if the woman Tim messed around with had gotten pregnant. Zach with a half sister or brother? Or your ex, when he cheated on you? I just can't believe my mother had a sibling she never knew about. Coleridge was already living in Shells Harbour when my mom died. They could have had a chance to know each other."

Penny realized Arlene was trying to ground herself, but the shock was heavy.

"All these secrets and lies, from everyone I know. My grandparents, my sister, my husband," Arlene said. She turned to face Penny squarely. "Even you, my best friend."

Penny felt her throat tighten. "What do you mean?"

"I've always wondered if you are ever going to tell me why you really left town."

"I left for university. You know that."

"But that doesn't explain why I never heard from you. At all. You just disappeared. I knew you were coming home for visits, but you never once called me."

Penny's stomach roiled. She turned away from Arlene for a moment as her breath tightened. "I couldn't, Arlene. I couldn't face you. I didn't want to."

"What did I ever do to you? We were best friends. I even went to Sheila about six months after you left to ask her if you were still alive."

"And Sheila wanted to tell you the truth. But I was too ashamed. I didn't want her to tell anyone and potentially ruin her name, her business."

"Tell anyone what?"

Penny turned back to Arlene and felt the first light flake of snow fall on her reddened cheeks. She thought about Mary's words, about Vicki's desire to flee Shells Harbour, flee the place that had been her only home. A town that had been cruel to her. Penny knew that urge to leave. She had done what Vicki longed to: leave everyone and everything in Shells Harbour behind her.

"It was my mother who slept with Vicki's boss, Panzer. And it was my mother who put the blame on Vicki. Delphine threw your sister to the wolves because she was having an affair with a married man and when she tried to convince him to leave his wife for her, he flat turned her down. She wanted to ruin his reputation by spreading an accusation about him being involved with a teenager."

Arlene glanced up at the heavy white sky before looking back at Penny.

"I know," she said. "I know all of it."

"You do? How?"

"I connected the dots later on when Vicki did a little investigating of her own, and Sheila confirmed it all after you had moved to Toronto," Arlene said. "Delphine had already gone back out west."

"She wanted to convince my father to take her back," Penny said. "As usual, that didn't go very well. I assume she's still in Red Deer. Dad's in Calgary."

"Vicki was so hurt by what happened," Arlene said. A light wind circled around the Lazy Pines parking lot, bringing more flakes of snow. "I was too, but I knew what your mother was capable of. You had told me plenty. I knew why it was Sheila who raised you. What I didn't know was that you'd leave town and never speak to me until you showed up on my doorstep last week. I can't believe you thought I wouldn't be able to see the difference between Delphine's lies, and our friendship."

Penny slumped back against the side of her car. If a sinkhole opened in the Lazy Pines parking lot, she would have considered diving in. For years, her guilt over the Panzer rumour kept her away from Arlene. But Arlene knew the whole time and was waiting for Penny to simply tell the truth.

"I should have stood up to her," Penny said. "I hated myself for what my mother did. For what it did to Vicki. I couldn't face you. I had just started my first year of university and Sheila came to Toronto for a visit. She told me that Delphine had admitted what she'd done, and that you and Vicki both knew. And she told me that Vicki tried-"

"Tried to take her own life?" Arlene finished the sentence that Penny couldn't. "She swallowed too many of the sleeping pills we still had in the bathroom from Mom's cancer treatment. It was Mary who found Vicki and called for help."

Penny stayed silent. Each word felt like a body blow. Delphine had used a teenage girl to escape from another mess she'd made. Back then Penny couldn't face Arlene, and especially not Vicki.

"I was so ashamed of Delphine," Penny said. "I still am. I want nothing to do with her."

"Disappearing made it so much worse," Arlene said. She shuffled her feet against the cold pavement and turned her pale face toward the sky in time to catch a fat snowflake on her nose. She looked back at Penny with the dust of snow lingering on her nose for a second before it fell to the pavement.

"I've had enough lies for a lifetime," she said, exhaling deeply. "Enough secrets. I missed you. I appreciate what you're doing for my sister and I'm sure Sheila is happy to have you back in town, but I'll be honest, Penny. We might not ever be like we were. Leenie and Peepee."

Penny nodded, shivering as if the cold had settled deeply into her bones. The stitches on her skull throbbed, and she swallowed the gulp of tears forming in her throat.

"I'm sorry for what my mother did, and what I did to you. If you choose to not speak to me again after we find out what happened to Vicki, I'll understand."

Penny squared up her shoulders and looked at Arlene. "But that's what matters to me now, and I know it matters to you," she said. "I should have asked McPhee whether the police have found Deana Simpson. I'm worried about her coming after you again."

"I told Tim he needs to talk to her. Tell her to back off. She'll communicate with him. Wherever she's hiding."

"At least we know she's not back at the house," Penny said. "Coleridge wouldn't have been there if she was too."

Arlene nodded, then paused for a moment.

"What if they actually were both there? At the same time?"

"Hiding out together? Deana and Coleridge? Why would they be hiding in Mary's house together?"

"Mary said Vicki first reached out to someone who identified as Annette Ross's granddaughter," Arlene said. "What if Deana Simpson is that woman? What if she's Coleridge's daughter?"

Penny thought about this. Deana and Coleridge had their similarities. They'd both appeared suddenly in Shells Harbour, although at different times. Deana conducted an audit at the fish plant, Prime Ocean. And had an affair with Arlene's husband that tore her family apart.

"That's a pretty big coincidence, don't you think? She got told to come here by her company, didn't she?"

"That's what Tim said. And maybe that's true. But maybe she wanted to be sent here."

It would have been an elaborate plan for Deana Simpson, and one that called into question her motive for having an affair with Tim. Penny now wondered if that was just a betrayal to pile on the pain to Vicki Truitt's family. A long plot of revenge for Mary's rejection of Annette Ross and a baby Coleridge.

"I take it Vicki gave you no hint about what she was doing, with the family research and looking for Annette Ross?"

Arlene shook her head. "I was clueless. Maybe I should see if I can get access to her messages. She might have saved some from the granddaughter." Arlene paused. "This all means I have a cousin out there somewhere. If I'm right, she played a big part in destroying my marriage, and knew exactly who she was sleeping with. And I also have an uncle. Who earlier today attacked one of my oldest friends."

"Are you sure these are people you want in your life? In Zach's?"

Arlene's phone chirped in her purse. She pulled it out and looked at the screen. "Zach wants Jared to come over after school. I won't say no to that," she said. "And when I drop him off later, I'll see if I can get on Vicki's laptop. As far as I know, Detective Sutton looked it over and handed it back to Roger." Arlene unlocked her car door, but paused before she got in. "And no, I don't think I want these people in my life. I can't see us having summer picnics and Christmas dinners together. But if they are key to finding out what happened to my sister, then so be it."

Penny nodded. At this point, she felt like she could offer no alternative for Arlene.

"Would you mind if I take the papers with me for the evening? Sheila's done some research into our family history, so she might have ideas about what's in the documents."

Arlene opened the back door to her SUV and pulled out the battered white banker's box. "It's all yours. I'll let you know if I get anywhere with Vicki's social media."

Penny slid the box into her car and waited until Arlene was out of the parking lot. For as long as her friend wanted her help, Penny would give it. Instead of turning left to head back toward town, she turned right, toward Hatchery Road.

Thirty

Penny slowed her car as she passed the entrance to Coleridge Coleman's trailer, but trees surrounded the narrow route, and she saw little from the road. She carried on past the driveway and turned left into the sprawling open dirt yard of Mariner's Sawmill. Even in the winter, the yard was busy. Workers had parked their cars in a row to the left, near the small building that held the office. To the right and back toward the woods, machines thrummed as they stripped and sawed trees trucked from the interior of the province.

The fishery built so many coastal towns in Nova Scotia, but the lumber industry wasn't far behind. And in Shells Harbour, Mariner's Sawmill was a place that nearly always needed workers, and applicants nearly always got a job, no questions asked.

Penny pulled open the door to the office building that looked like a converted shipping container and stepped inside. Tim Tanner shuffled through a stack of papers in a back corner of the office.

Tim had grown a beard since the pictures of him as a clean-shaven young father appeared on Arlene's social media. Those photos were how Penny kept track of her old friend, saw her get married, buy a home and build a family, even when she was too guilt-ridden to be a part of her world.

Now, those pictures were gone from Arlene's profile and so was the happy father. His identity changed into a tired, middle-aged man who might have been trying to melt into the background of the town. If that was the case, Penny wouldn't blame him. He had made a series of terrible decisions, bringing destruction into his marriage that bled into his whole life. The village would be merciless in making him feel it. A back corner of Mariner's Sawmill with a dark beard and a puffy vest to ward against the chill in the shipping container-turned office was probably the best thing he could do, short of skipping town altogether.

"Can I help you?" Tim looked up from his papers toward the front desk. Penny guessed a receptionist might have been there if it wasn't so late in the afternoon.

"I'm Penny Pintz. A friend of Arlene's."

"You're Penny?" Tim got up from his chair and moved toward the counter that separated the back of the office from the front. "Arlene used to tell me stories about her friend Penny. I thought you lived in Toronto."

Penny smiled, despite everything. She was coming to regret the years she snuck home to Shells Harbour and had short visits with Sheila before sliding out again, breathing with relief as Nova Scotia receded below her airplane window in a shadow of forests.

Meanwhile, Arlene built a family life in Shells Harbour that Tim had brought to ruin. As it turned out, that destruction took place around the same time Penny's own life in Toronto was imploding, and Shells Harbour became her only choice for refuge. Not that Tim would learn that much detail about her life. She replied simply, telling him she'd recently moved home. But there was the lingering memory of Callum, and his own betrayal. That wound was still fresh enough that any mention of the city brought him to mind, and a twinge of pain.

Tim led Penny behind the counter and pulled some papers off an upholstered chair that looked like it belonged in a church basement. Penny told him she was trying to help Arlene discover who killed Vicki, and why.

"And right now, we're trying to find out if there's a connection to Deana," she said. Tim's arm made a light swoosh as it brushed against his vest when he put his hand to his cheek. He rubbed his beard stubble. Penny held his stare for a moment, before politely breaking to give him time to process her words. She glanced through a dirty windowpane into the lumberyard. An echo of machinery gave a backdrop of noise.

"I'll be honest with you," Tim said finally. "I've been covering up so much and lying so much that my first reaction is to tell you as little as possible."

"I suppose I can understand that," Penny said. "But I'd like to know why a woman attacked Arlene and me at the Barkson house on Outcrop Road."

"You were attacked? Is Arlene okay?"

Penny nodded and gave Tim a quick version of the fire and the fight, feeling her own instinct to keep some details private from the man who'd hurt Arlene. Tim asked if she knew who set the fire and carried out the attack.

"I have a feeling you already know who did it," Penny said. "At least on some level. You must have known what she was capable of when you tossed your life up in the air for her."

"You're saying Deana attacked you?" Tim shook his head. "I didn't think she was capable of that kind of violence. It must be some kind of jealousy. Delusions that she could scare me back into her life," he said. "What have the police told you?"

"Not much, and I haven't spoken to them about who did it," Penny said. "That's my problem. And Arlene and Roger's problem. I'm only here talking to you because the police seem to be uninterested in anything other than parking tickets." Wally McPhee flashed into Penny's mind and she wondered how long the eager officer would stay on a force like the SHPD, if they didn't promote him to detective as he hoped. "I have to ask, did Deana ever talk to you about Vicki?"

Tim looked at Penny with tired brown eyes. She could see that he wanted to talk. She hoped he calculated that with his lost marriage, job and home, at least he could try to salvage some respect by helping Penny give Arlene peace. He offered a nod.

"When Mary moved into Lazy Pines, we left a lot of her papers in a locked bedroom. Arlene planned to sort through them later but hadn't gotten around to it by the time Deana came to town," Tim said. "You know she was renting the house while she was working on the audit for my company?"

Penny nodded, leaning forward to encourage him on.

"One day I went over there and the bedroom door was open. Deana wasn't expecting me, and I found her with Mary's papers all out of the boxes and files, tossed all over the place."

"Did you ask her why?"

Tim nodded. "She got incredibly flustered." Penny had a hard time picturing the woman who had slammed her skull and wrestled Arlene getting flustered, but she kept quiet as Tim carried on. "She made up an excuse about looking for some spare blankets for her bed, but she would have had to pick the lock on the door to get into the room. I should have pushed her harder, but I dropped it. Chalked it up to being nosy."

Tim looked out the grimy window to the yard and shook his head slowly, as if he was too tired to move any faster. Shells Harbour in the late winter seemed like a town filled with people exhausted under the weight of secrets that were coming into the light.

Except one. Someone in the town was a killer, and that was a secret still hidden.

"Can you tell me why she was auditing your company in the first place?"

"I started working at Prime Ocean a few years ago in accounting. It took me a while to get up to speed on the books, but I could see corners were being cut. We had new management, and I took my concerns to them. They contracted Deana's company in the city to do an independent audit and she came down."

"What corners were being cut?" Penny wasn't sure she could draw Tim on that. She knew from Arlene the company was still investigating the whole matter, but she wanted to know more about what Deana Simpson was doing in town.

"I suppose I can tell you. They can't fire me twice, right?" Tim said with a bitter chuckle. "I saw a lot of suppliers overcharging. A lot of times, the product we received was less than what we should have been getting. Frankly, the company was paying a high price and getting crap in return."

Penny nodded, while thinking that the fraud Tim was describing sounded a lot like what seemed to be going on at the Winter Carnival.

"It's easy enough to hide when you control the supply chain," Tim said.

"What happened with Deana's audit?"

Tim pushed himself up from his desk. He crossed the short space to a humming water cooler and filled a grungy-looking bottle from his desk. He took a long drink before offering Penny a paper cup. She shook her head and gave him time to gather himself before he carried on.

"By this point, we were already involved," he said. "In hindsight, that's one thing that surprises me the most. How quickly I threw my marriage down the toilet. She had been with the company for less than a month and things were tense around the office. People in our procurement department didn't like her asking questions, so I was told to act as her liaison. Get her the documents she needed and all."

The front door to the trailer banged open and three men in coveralls coated with sawdust pounded in. One of them offered an acknowledgement to Tim and Penny as they each grabbed their timecards from slots on the wall and punched themselves out of work. Tim nodded back as the workers stepped out into the rest of their day. The trailer fell silent again, and Tim continued.

"Deana would get the documents and she'd go through them and prepare some reports. But there were things that seemed beyond her grasp, like how companies can write off certain assets and defer payments. Basic things anyone into corporate accounts should know," he said. "I spoke to her company in Halifax and brought up some of the issues I was seeing. They admitted she was on her first assignment alone."

"Seems like a big job for someone with little experience," Penny said.

"That's what I thought too. I asked her boss in the city why they sent her out here and he told me she'd pushed hard for it. I had a feeling he couldn't say no to her."

Penny raised her eyebrows. "For the same reason you couldn't?"

Tim nodded. "That's my guess, anyway." He took another long sip of his water. "That's when I knew I needed to end it. And when I tried, she went to my boss. But that backfired on her. He axed me and threatened Deana's company with a lawsuit unless she was fired, too."

"So that's when it all came out," Penny said. "What I'm still wondering is, why was Deana so keen to come to Shells Harbour in the first place?"

"I don't know. She always seemed curious about Mary and Albert, though, even before I found her in the bedroom that time. She'd stare at photos of older family members on the walls of the Barkson house, and pictures of Mary and Albert from a long time ago," Tim said. "I couldn't shake the feeling she was still snooping even after I caught her. I thought in some strange way she was curious about my wife."

"But maybe Deana wanted to know about the whole Barkson family," Penny said. "If she's still trying to contact you, would you be willing to speak with her?"

Tim shook his head. "I need to cut her off. Completely. What if she attacks again? She could come after Arlene, or even Zach. She knows I have a son. My marriage might be over, but I have no desire to be around a woman like Deana. I still can't believe she attacked you and Arlene just to get at me."

"Tim, that might not have been about you. In fact, I'm not sure any of this is about you. I think this is all connected to Arlene, Vicki and their family," Penny said.

Penny churned through the information she'd gathered. Tim seemed as much in the dark as she was about Deana's true motives, and nervous about the very idea of speaking with her. Although given her behaviour, he had good reason to be worried.

Penny wanted to spend more time scouring the papers in the box in her car, the same ones Deana had been digging through herself, as well as the documents that Coleridge said belonged to him. She pushed herself up from Tim's desk and headed for the door before an idea stopped her. She turned back to him.

"Are you planning to go to the hockey game?"

"The police and firefighters' game for the carnival? Yeah, I take Zach every year," Tim replied. "I expect we'll have Jared with us too. Sounds like he's practically living with Arlene now. And he could probably use the distraction."

"It's tomorrow night, right?"

Tim nodded. "The carnival starts in the afternoon with the kids' play day, then the hockey game at night."

"And I assume everyone in town goes to the game, right?"

"Oh yeah, absolutely. It always packs the rink," he said. Tim folded his arms across his chest. "What are you thinking?"

"I think that everyone in town might include Deana Simpson. And it might also include whoever killed Vicki Truitt."

Thirty-One

Penny called Jacob when she left Mariner's Sawmill. The hospital discharged him with stitches and a heavy bandage on his cut arm. He was about to stop by the police station to give a statement to Wally McPhee. And Penny suspected he might ask a few questions of his own, to see if the young police officer learned anything new from Coleridge.

"If Deana is Coleridge's daughter, that makes her related to Arlene," Jacob said after Penny explained what they learned from Mary, and what they now suspected. "And Vicki."

"Tim doesn't know where Deana is, but I have a feeling she's still around," Penny said. "Tomorrow night, at the hockey game, be careful. Tim's going to have Zach and Jared there. We don't know how far Deana's willing to go."

Jacob said he'd try to track down a photo of Deana online and ask a few of the other firefighters to watch out for her. "You need to be careful too," he said. "You and Arlene. If Deana attacked you once, she might come back."

Penny cradled the banker's box of papers in her right arm and tugged open the door to Brittle Pages with her left. The warm smell of the bookstore, quiet in the waning hour of Sheila's business day, comforted Penny immediately. Out in the town, Penny was on guard. Wally had arrested Coleridge for the attack on Jacob and Chris, but Deana was still floating around somewhere. Penny had a feeling Jacob could be right. Deana Simpson wasn't done with Shells Harbour yet.

Sheila appeared from a back corner of the bookstore, hidden under a long, woven poncho style cover-up. She swished to Penny's side and helped her close the door against a steady fall of snow.

"What do we have here?" she asked as Penny plunked the box on the front counter. Sheila turned over the open sign to signal that Brittle Pages was shut for the evening and followed Penny into the kitchen to put the kettle on for tea.

There was no way for Penny to soothe Sheila's nerves as she recounted Coleridge's appearance at the Barkson house. Sheila shook her head.

"Never would have thought he'd be capable of violence," she said. "He's always just been the quiet man around town, keeping to himself."

"I'm still cringing at how it felt to hit him in the stomach with that rolling pin." Penny let out a shudder. Coleridge was a thin man, and she knew her strike would have connected sharply with some vital organs. But with him standing near a bleeding Jacob, Penny wanted a debilitating blow.

"If Arlene was protecting Chris and calling for help, Jacob needed you to do something. You had no choice," Sheila said. "Well, you had a choice. You could have not gotten involved with this nonsense in the first place. Once again, I'll remind you that you're not a police officer."

"I know I'm not, but it's pretty damning when Wally said he's following me around because I'm making more headway than his own detective."

Sheila let out one of her loud sighs that let Penny knew she had conceded the point, but wasn't pleased about it. Instead, she reached behind Penny and placed two chipped mugs on the counter to pour streams of hot water over herbal tea bags. The kitchen smelled of raspberry.

"So, what's this, then?" Sheila said, as they looked at the box of papers back in the store. She might have warned Penny against getting involved, but she was clearly interested in the contents.

"I hope these are answers," Penny said. She wanted the documents to offer some clues that could draw a line to Vicki's death, and a killer she could hand over to Wally.

Penny slid next to Sheila. They pored over the documents, a

haphazard collection of receipts for appliances bought many years earlier, newspaper clippings about local events that had caught Mary or Albert's eye for reasons that weren't obvious to Penny or Sheila. There were bank records of the kind they had discovered at the house that showed payments made by Mary to Annette Ross, but most of those records showed transactions in cash.

"That was, of course, the norm back then," Sheila said. "Took cash from the bank and paid for everything that way."

"Not everything," Penny said, pulling a file from the box. "Here's an IOU from Mary and Albert, but I can't make out the signature at the bottom. It's for $5,000."

Sheila looked at the paper over Penny's shoulder. "That looks like a C, and some scribbles. And maybe another C."

"CC? Who do we know that has those initials?"

Sheila laid a finger on the letters, as if trying to bring them to life. "You know the only one that I do. It certainly might be Coleridge Coleman. Look at the date. September 15, 1993. I can't say for sure, but I think that's around when he moved to Shells Harbour. And I'd bet that would be about the value of his land there by Mariner's at the time."

"Do you think Mary and Albert loaned Coleridge money for his land? Right here in Shells Harbour. After all those years of trying to keep him and his mother away from this town."

"Albert would have been in his 70s, by then," Sheila said. "Maybe he wanted to have his only son closer to him."

"But this says IOU. Coleman must have intended to pay it back," Penny said. She reached back into a manilla folder and pulled out more papers. They were carbon copies of receipts for amounts in a few hundred dollars each, stretching over several years through the 1990s.

"These are all made out to Mary and Albert. Down here in the note line it says CC." Penny squinted to read the signatures on each receipt, signed in a different hand than the first invoice. "These are all signed by Erin Riggings!"

"Erin? Why on earth would she be paying off a loan for Coleridge Coleman?"

"Erin's involved in all this, somehow," Penny said. "I'm sure of it. She's got her fingers all over the carnival, and we know she and Vicki didn't get along. Roger said someone might have faked Vicki's signature on cheques that needed signing to pay suppliers. Erin would have had access to all that, and Vicki probably didn't realize what was happening because she was distracted by the things she found out about her family."

"But where does Erin fit in with the Barksons?"

Outside of Brittle Pages' front window, Barque Lane settled into the late winter dusk as the town calmed. Shells Harbour wasn't a place with a heady nightlife, but the pub would soon serve warm bowls of Irish stew and local ale. Tourists would tuck into fish and chips at the Harbourfront Diner. There would be a junior hockey game at the rink, which would be getting ready for the big face-off between the emergency responders. And the Winter Carnival committee, without Vicki Truitt, would be putting the finishing touches on the games and displays at the community centre for the kickoff event.

Sheila turned back to Penny. "Vicki was trying to fulfil Mary's wish about finding her grandfather's son, who was here the whole time. Which Mary clearly knew. But it still doesn't explain why Erin was paying a debt for Coleridge in the 1990s."

Penny turned back to the box and pulled out another group of newspaper clippings. They were yellowed and felt ready to fall apart in her fingers. She gingerly placed the pages on the sales counter and leaned over them. In a corner, an advertisement glowed about a new type of instant coffee.

"This ad is for a grocery store in the Valley," Penny said. "There are a lot of clippings of papers out there. That's two hours away."

Sheila turned back to Penny and looked over her shoulder. She tapped a dense column of type that Penny's eyes had skipped.

"Do you know what this is? We used to have it in the papers here too. This was the original social media."

"Neighbours and Notes," Penny said, reading the title of the column of text. "What is it?"

"Back in the day, every village had a community member write up the comings and goings of their neighbourhood. Who travelled where, who had a visitor from out of town. What meetings were held and who got married or had a death in the family."

"That seems a little nosy."

"No more so than those things you look at on your phone," Sheila said. Penny had to concede that to her aunt. "I bet there's a reason why Mary Barkson kept these clippings."

Penny laid a finger on one of the papers and peered at the small type.

"Henry and Abigail Dickerson of Bridgetown received Stanley and Gladys Pyke from Truro for a weekend visit, where they attended supper and a bingo at the Bridgetown Legion," Penny read out loud. "Wow. That's detailed."

Sheila nodded and kept reading to herself for a moment. Penny didn't recognize any of the names in the pieces she had, and the locations were well over an hour's drive from Shells Harbour.

"Wait a second," Sheila said, her voice low before she perked up. "Listen to this. Annette Walker and her son David Ross-Walker of Middleton travelled to Halifax to visit family for the holiday week," she said. "Annette Walker could be Annette Ross."

"Maybe she got married. Who's David? Did she have two sons?" Penny began looking at her section of the paper for the Walker name. "Here's one, from May 1968. Gerald and Annette Walker are pleased to announce the birth of their daughter, Katherine Walker. Annette had a second child."

"Katherine?" Sheila asked. "1968? She'd be about 50 now. You know what's a nickname for Katherine?"

Penny thought for a moment before looking up from the newspaper. "Kathy? Katie?"

Sheila shook her head. "It's not as common as it used to be, but I had a friend at university whose full name was Katherine. She went by Erin. It's not heard a lot around here but my friend was from the Valley too. Might be more common out there."

"Erin as a nickname for Katherine? As in, Erin Riggings?"

Sheila nodded. "She would be about the right age. She always said she moved to Shells Harbour after her husband got a job at Prime Ocean. I never really asked where she came from because she just slid into our lives like she was here all along."

"So, who's David to her? And why did Erin Riggings pay debt for Coleridge Coleman?"

"Katherine Walker wasn't the only person in that family to start a new life in Shells Harbour. Coleridge would be in his mid-50s, a couple years older than Erin," Sheila said, taking a long pause. "I think David is Coleridge."

"They're brother and sister," Penny said, exhaling the breath she was holding in. "And she moved him over here and bought him land. And all those years, Mary Barkson was keeping tabs on the family through the community notices."

"Just like we all do now with our phones," Sheila said.

"But what kind of name is Coleridge? If he's the same person as David Ross, where did that come from?"

"Coleridge. You know, people out in the Valley say there's a part of the mountain that looks as dark as coal when the sun sets on it, a place they called the Coal Ridge. It wouldn't be too far from Middleton. Maybe David wanted to keep a piece of his hometown with him when he moved."

Penny slid the newspaper clippings back into the folder and considered her next moves. She'd need to tell Jacob and Arlene. Erin Riggings wasn't a potential direct beneficiary of the Barkson home if it sold, but her half-brother Coleridge would be, according to Mary's rules. Erin could be using him. Perhaps buying the land for his trailer wasn't simply a favour, and she was now trying to call in some of the debt she'd paid off years earlier.

"You said Erin and her husband moved to town so he could work at the fish plant?"

Sheila nodded. "Early 90s, if I recall. You were still in elementary school. He retired last summer."

"Retired? Is he much older than Erin?"

"Maybe a few years, not by much. But I'm sure she was in here talking about Ward retiring to open a sail-making shop on the waterfront. Was a big dream of his, she said."

"Right, Sail Away," Penny said. "Do you know what he did at Prime Ocean?"

Sheila thought about that. "I'm trying to remember what Erin would go on about," she said. "Procurement, maybe? Yes, supply chain stuff. Cause I'd talk about my issues getting books shipped here from Toronto or Montreal and she'd say, 'oh that's nothing, you should hear what Ward has to go through to get that Russian fish they make at the plant now'."

"Russian fish?"

"Apparently they get a lot of imported fish, despite the fact that we live on the ocean," Sheila said with a shrug that sent one shoulder of her woven poncho sliding out of place. "It's not the same as it once was."

"Tim said that's what Deana was sent here to audit, after his complaint about procurement," Penny said. "Like a larger scale version of what Esi and Tammy said was going on at the carnival."

Penny's phone rang in her shoulder bag. She rushed to grab it and glanced at the screen before answering. "Hey Arlene, what's going on?"

"Penny, I was right," she said forcefully, like the words were about to burst out from her. "Deana is Coleridge's daughter. Vicki had it all figured out. I can see it here on her laptop. She connected all the dots."

"Arlene, I'm here with Sheila and we've got some things to tell you too, I'm going to put you on speaker."

"Okay. When I dropped Jared off tonight, I started talking to Roger. I wanted to keep him in the loop about what we've found out."

"Good idea."

"Roger said he'd been looking through more of Vicki's papers. She'd been researching for months," Arlene said. "Roger told me Vicki spent a week out in the Valley, tracking down old phone books and records."

"Did she find Annette?"

"Yes! Well, she found Annette's burial site. I have pictures of it. She died ten years ago, but apparently in her later life she got quite involved in the Rotary. Vicki found a copy of a monthly newsletter with pictures from the funeral service the club held for her."

"That's amazing," Penny said. As Arlene continued talking, Penny unraveled her thoughts about Vicki. As it turned out, she might not have grown from troubled teen to become a doctor's wife and community leader, who had a side job in pocketing cash from the carnival committee. If Vicki's bid to find all of Albert's heirs was to convince Mary to sell the house in order to flee Shells Harbour, she might have unleashed a nest of hornets instead.

"It's grainy, but there's someone in there who looks a whole lot like Deana might have a decade ago."

Penny heard the telling sound of Arlene slamming a car door and the beep of her remote lock. "You're never going to guess what we found out too, Leenie," Penny said.

"Don't tell me. I'm going to run inside and check on Zach, and then I'll head over. I think we're finally figuring this all out."

"Zach's not home," Penny said. "Tim's taking him to the police versus fire carnival hockey game tonight."

Arlene was silent for a moment, and Penny could feel her friend's curiosity. "I went to the sawmill. I wanted to ask Tim about Deana."

"Ah," Arlene replied simply. "Well, I'll just change out of my office clothes and I'll be over in 20 minutes."

Penny told Arlene they were closing Brittle Pages, and they'd be home shortly. Penny and Sheila replaced the papers in the banker's box and they switched off the lights to head home and wait for Arlene.

Thirty-Two

Penny looked at the schooner-shaped wall clock over Sheila's stove. She checked against her phone that showed the time of Arlene's call. Her friend had said 20 minutes, but almost 45 had passed since they spoke.

"I'll try her again," Penny said. But the call rang a handful of times before clicking to voicemail. Sheila poured another stream of hot water into the teapot and looked at Penny with her brows pinched together.

"This isn't like her, is it?"

Penny shook her head. "Arlene is so punctual, you could set a clock by her. I did tell her about the hockey game. Maybe that upset her. I'll call Jacob and see if she's at the rink."

It took several rings before Jacob answered his phone and when he did, the din of a noisy hockey crowd beat against his words.

"Hang on, Penny. I'll step outside," he shouted into his phone. Penny listened as the echo of cheers faded. "That's better. What were you asking?"

"Has Arlene come to the rink?"

"I don't think so," Jacob said. "Zach and Jared are sitting behind our bench and I didn't see Arlene with them."

Penny looked at Sheila and shook her head. She gave Jacob a quick rundown of the situation and what they had found, including Arlene's discovery about Deana's connection to Coleridge.

"Wait, Erin Riggings is Coleridge's sister? And his real name is

David? And the woman who slept with Arlene's husband is Coleridge's daughter?"

"Yeah, that about sums it up," Penny said. "Arlene should have been here by now."

"Meet me at her house," Jacob said. "I can get us in if necessary. Firefighters have ways, but don't tell anyone I said that."

Penny chuckled, grateful for a bit of levity that still did little to ease her rippling anxiety for Arlene. "Do you see Tim there?"

"I might have seen him earlier. It's hard to tell. This place is packed, must be half the town in here."

"Well, don't mention anything to the boys yet," Penny said. "No need to worry them if it's nothing. She's been burning the candle at both ends, so we might just find her snoozing on her couch."

But Penny knew as soon as she pulled up to the curb in front of Arlene's bungalow, that wouldn't be the case. As Penny stepped out from her car into the dark, snowy street, she saw Arlene's black leather purse laying in the snow. Again, she pulled out her phone to try her friend, and her stomach churned as she realized the sing-song ringtone was coming from her feet. Arlene's cell phone was on the ground, under a layer of fresh snow.

Jacob's pickup truck pulled in behind Penny's smaller car. By the time he approached, Penny was struggling to quell a growing sense of panic. Her breath rose in short, shallow gasps.

"She's not here Jacob," Penny said. "Where's her car? Where the hell is she?"

Jacob grasped Penny's arms and held her still. "Breathe," he said. "We need to stay calm if we're going to find her. I'll go check the house."

Jacob walked up the path to the side door and peered through the window. He tried the door and began looking under rocks for hidden keys. "I thought I should try the official way before we go the firefighter way," he said as Penny appeared behind him with Arlene's snowy purse and phone. He pulled a small metal tool from a flat box he carried in his hand, and Penny was astonished to see how quickly he clicked open the lock on Arlene's door.

"You didn't see me do that," Jacob said. They slipped into the house, cool and dark in the winter evening. Penny wiped the snow from her boots and moved to the living room, still hoping she'd see her friend sleeping soundly on the couch.

But it was empty, with a plaid blanket folded neatly underneath a throw cushion. She looked in Arlene's bedroom as well as Zach's. Both were empty. The house was still.

"She's not here," Penny said. "We should call the police."

"Every member of the Shells Harbour Police Department is at the rink right now," Jacob said. "That kid who came out to the Barkson house is the only one left on duty."

"Wally McPhee? Call him. He's the only cop interested in this case anyway," Penny said. Jacob nodded, pulling out his phone as they left the house and relocked the door. Penny sent Sheila a quick message to let her know Arlene wasn't there.

Nearly everyone in Shells Harbour was at the hockey game in the rink or curled up in their quiet homes on one of the last snowy nights of the season. Penny looked around Arlene's neighbourhood, at the wisps of chimney smoke lifting into the early moonrise. Penny couldn't believe Arlene had simply walked away from her home.

No, she was gone, and it wasn't by her choice. Someone had taken her. Penny signalled to get Jacob's attention.

"Tell Wally to meet us at the Barkson house," she said. "That's what this has been about all along."

Penny and Jacob followed each other, driving through the quiet streets to the edge of town where the Atlantic Ocean battered against a rock wall separating the road from the waves. In stormy weather, the road would often flood, sending salty shoots of water slapping against the windows of passing cars. On this night, the storm had settled, but the waves were still churning.

Penny led the way, and Jacob was close behind in his truck. Like most trips in Shells Harbour, it was only a drive of a few minutes, but Penny forced herself to creep along the snowy road. She needed to get there in one piece.

Around a sharp curve, the Barkson house appeared through the grove of trees that surrounded it. Its sturdiness towered over the roiling ocean. Penny whipped her car into the driveway and didn't allow herself time to think about the memories she had made in that house, the warm sleepovers with Arlene where Vicki would ask to be let into their fun. Mary was there for many of their long talks and Penny now knew the house held Mary's secrets, the ones that weighed on her marriage and her family.

The ones that were now coming home.

Her headlights scanned the back window as she put her car in park. Jacob was immediately behind her. She feared her assumption about where Arlene was taken might have been wrong until she saw a tidy blue compact car tucked at the far edge of the driveway. And Arlene's grey SUV beside it.

"Did you get hold of Wally?" Penny said quietly to Jacob as they surveyed the house.

"Had to leave him a couple messages. Texted him too. If he's in the rink watching the game, he probably wouldn't hear his phone ringing," Jacob said. Penny exhaled. They were alone, and there would be no help to come. Penny motioned to the car.

"I don't know who's driving that. Could be Deana." The swoop of their headlights coming into the yard would have already given them away to whoever was hiding in the darkened house, and they decided to go inside.

Penny's heart thudded as they approached the house. They slid past the ornate front door to the kitchen entrance off the patio, where the charred box of decorations still sat. Jacob turned the knob and slipped in, Penny on his heels.

From the kitchen, Penny saw the foyer was empty of the coats and boots that would normally clutter the entrance to a Shells Harbour home in the winter. This house, though, should have been cold and quiet.

But it wasn't. They walked toward the living room, where a flicker of flames reflected in the darkened picture window. For an instant Penny thought the house was on fire, but it was just the glow of the fireplace and a warm hearth.

And against the flickering light, Penny gasped, seeing Arlene in a corner, a white bandana shoved through her clenched teeth and her hands bound behind her back. A piece of paper and a pen were on the wooden floor in front of her.

Penny rushed to her friend and struggled to untie the knotted fabric at the back of her head. Jacob had crossed through the living room and left again in the second entrance. Penny's fingers loosened the bandana, and she pulled the gag from Arlene's mouth.

"It's Deana, Penny, she did it all," Arlene said as Penny worked the rope tying her hands together. "She killed Vicki."

"Did she grab you tonight?"

Arlene nodded, rubbing the back of her head. "Came up behind me and whacked me with something. Knocked me right out and threw me in the back of my own car. The thing is, Penny, she wasn't alone."

"What do you mean?"

"There was someone else there," Arlene said, her hands fighting against the knot as Penny struggled with it. "I don't know who it was."

"I think you do, though."

Penny finally wormed her finger into the core of the knot that was holding Arlene's hands together when the new voice stopped her short.

They both looked toward the entrance of the living room, where a pair had emerged from the hallway toward the light of the fire.

"My God," Arlene gasped. "Tim, what have you done?"

Thirty-Three

Arlene's husband stepped out from the darkness with a black hand-gun pointed at Jacob, who carefully moved along with him. Penny saw Deana Simpson emerge on the other side, with a tight grip on Jacob's arm. She had thin strands of blond hair framing her gaunt face and Penny could see she was a woman ready for a fight, with whatever strength she had in her.

Arlene shook out her wrists, but Penny could tell the pain in her friend's hands was nothing like what she was feeling toward her husband. Arlene's eyes narrowed.

"Are you finally going to sign the papers?" Tim gestured to the document on the floor in front of where he had restrained his wife.

"What the hell are you doing?" Arlene yelled, pushing herself up to her feet. But Deana wouldn't let her get that far.

"Back on the ground," she spat out. Arlene backed away but didn't kneel down to the woman who'd slept with her husband. And killed her sister. Penny knew her friend would defy every one of Deana's commands. Instead, Arlene perched on the edge of the couch covered in a dusty white drop cloth.

Penny's mind churned. Tim Tanner and Arlene were still married. Separated and living apart, but Arlene had told Penny they were going to therapy to work out parenting plans for Zach.

She thought, too, about her conversation hours earlier with Tim at the sawmill. He'd played her well, acting like a remorseful, bewildered husband swept up by Deana. She had told him too much, and he'd used it to attack Arlene.

"I can't believe you're taking the side of the woman who tried to kill the mother of your child," Penny said, her voice dripping with disgust as the memory of Deana choking Arlene in the snow surfaced.

"Deana says you attacked her first," Tim replied, and the woman on his side nodded quickly.

"That's a complete lie, Tim," Arlene said, making a motion to take a step forward but wobbling back a half step, still dazed from the blow to her head. Penny jumped forward to catch Arlene while Deana yelped.

"Everyone just calm down," Jacob said, wincing as Tim nudged him further into the living room by pushing his gun into the bandage that covered the wound on his arm from Coleridge's slash.

"This can't be happening," Arlene said, shaking her head. "We spent years together. We have a child together. What's Zach going to say about all this?"

"He'll love it when you give me the money from this house and I can buy him anything he wants. Sign the papers, my dear. Give me your rights to this land and we'll all walk out of here."

"Zach doesn't care about stuff, Tim. He never has. He just wanted to spend time with his father. He wanted to make you proud."

Tim scoffed. "He's a teenage boy. He's going to love walking into school with the cool sneakers and that new phone he's been begging for. And he could have had it already if you and Vicki weren't clinging to this place."

Arlene shook her head. "That's a load of crap," she said, the tension in her voice mounting. Penny raised her eyebrows at her friend, but Arlene didn't see the look of warning. Tim had pushed Jacob nearer to them while he and Deana stood by the fireplace, its flames providing the only light in the room.

"This is about more than getting Zach some sneakers and a phone and whatever else you think you can use to buy your son's love," Arlene said. She looked closely at Deana, whose green eyes and hair were back lit by the fire, making her pale skin turn pinkish. "What's she got you into? Do you know she killed Vicki?"

"You're just as crazy as Tim always said you were. I didn't kill anyone."

Arlene let the insult slide and pressed on. "You must have forgotten whispering that after you two shoved me in the backseat of my car. Maybe you thought I was unconscious, but I assure you, I heard every disgusting word of what you did to my sister. You shouldn't have left her alone with me, Tim."

"I had to pick the boys up and take them to the rink," he said, casting a quick glance to Deana, who glared only at Arlene.

Penny put a hand on Arlene's back to comfort her. They'd have to work through it later, but right now, the gun clutched in Tim's hand was her focus. She couldn't tell if it was loaded, but judging by the way his wrist sagged, it was heavy and his control of the weapon wasn't sharp. He was still the tired-looking shell of a man she saw earlier at the sawmill. But with the quick look he gave Deana as Arlene spoke, Penny wondered how in sync they really were.

Deana crossed her arms over her chest like an angry child. The nylon red jacket she wore on top of a thin black sweater with blue piping made a light shush as she shuffled. The sweater matched that worn by the figure on the trail when Coleridge's home burned. With Vicki dead inside.

"I think I know what this is really about," Penny said. "It all goes back to Prime Ocean, doesn't it? The audit. You know exactly what happened to the money."

"No, I don't," Tim said, his voice climbing. "I knew something was wrong. That's why I called for the audit. But I have told everyone over and over again I don't know where the money went."

"Actually, I wasn't talking to you, Tim," Penny said, shifting her look to his right. "This is all about her."

Deana tried to protest, but Penny spoke over her. She needed to drive a wedge between Deana and Tim, who shifted his grip awkwardly on the sagging gun.

"No, we're done with your lies, Deana," she said, keeping her voice as steady as she could. "You've torn at least two families apart, all because you never had your own."

"You have no idea what you're talking about," the woman sputtered, raking a thin hand through her scraggly hair.

Penny scoffed. "I don't? You think I don't know what it's like to have a messed-up family? My father left my mother, and she ran all over this town, cheating and chasing after everything she could get her hands on. And, as it turned out, I inherited her skill for turning her back on people who loved her."

Jacob cast a questioning look at Penny, but Arlene nodded her support and Penny continued. "Family doesn't mean that you share DNA. Family is who stands by you, no matter what."

"What a joke," Deana said. "Family doesn't mean a thing."

"Except it does. And all of this is about who your family is, Deana. We know exactly who you are. Deana Simpson. Daughter of David Ross, granddaughter of Annette Walker. And of Albert Barkson."

"Which makes you my cousin," Arlene said. Her winter-pale face showed hints of colour as her strength returned. Deana's eyes grew wide at first, but she quickly turned defiant and squared her narrow shoulders toward Arlene.

"That's damn right. And that makes me just as entitled to a say in what happens to this house as you, cousin."

Arlene ignored her and turned to her husband, now holding the gun limply by his side, his finger on the trigger guard and his swagger sucked away.

"Did you know all this when you got mixed up with her?"

He shook his head. "Not right away. But I knew she had a difficult life and had been finding some things out recently."

"Recently? Well, this is what Vicki found out, and it probably got her killed. And I might have been next if I refused to sign the papers. Deana, you were a foster kid, weren't you?"

The woman turned her back to Arlene, facing the fireplace with her arms folded. Arlene focused back on Tim.

"She was in the system from a young age after her mother died. Car accident, and the cops suspected drinking. With little Deana asleep in the back. But at some point, little Deana grew up and went looking for her father. David Ross. Who Shells Harbour knows as Coleridge Coleman, the recluse who lives in a junkyard."

"And in a trailer that you set on fire, didn't you?" Penny added, turning to Deana, who still refused to acknowledge her or Arlene. "I saw you on the trail right after. Wearing the same sweater you have on right now. I called the fire department, but I think we both know that Vicki was already dead, wasn't she?"

Tim used his free hand to grab Deana and whirl her around to face him.

"You killed Arlene's sister? For a bigger piece of this land?"

Deana shook her arm loose, and Penny saw the fire reflecting in her eyes. It seemed as though she was being consumed by her own flames. Penny saw a flash of the anger that brought violence to Vicki, a blow to the head delivered probably by a hammer Coleridge certainly would have had around his ramshackle property.

"My father has more rights to this land than anyone. He's the direct heir of Albert Barkson and this should be his. Not that disgusting trailer in the woods," Deana said. "Vicki should have just signed over the rights and so should you."

"So what happened? Did Vicki put it all together?" Jacob asked. "Did she reach out to talk to you and you lured her to the trailer? The final text message she got was from someone arranging a meeting with her. That was you, wasn't it?"

His words didn't yet sway Deana. Jacob continued. "We know a blow to the head killed Vicki. Based on what the medical examiner told us, you're just the right height for the strike that ended her life."

"My father let me stay with him after you kicked me out of here," Deana said to Tim. "Out of a house that should be mine and his." Her tone shifted to a plea, and she grabbed Tim's free hand. "She came at me first, I swear." She looked at him with wide eyes and Penny thought for a moment he would fall for it.

"We've heard that one before," Penny said with a scoff.

"And you set the trailer on fire, thinking it would hide the evidence of what you did," Jacob said to Deana. "Except Penny called 9-1-1, and we put it out much sooner than you expected. Vicki's body was practically untouched by the fire."

"I didn't mean for all this to happen," Deana said, still focused on Tim. But he stayed silent and let go of her.

"You don't believe me? Fine. You spineless man. You were so easy to seduce. I was almost embarrassed for you." Deana turned to Arlene. "It was so simple to turn your family upside down, just like your grandmother did to mine."

Penny knew what was going to happen the instant Arlene stepped forward. She grabbed a fistful of Deana's hair and tossed her to the floor. Tim raised the gun, but Jacob lunged and knocked Tim's hand backward, smashing his wrist into the brick hearth and sending the weapon tumbling to the floor.

Penny looked between the two, unsure where to step in. Deana scrabbled against Arlene, trying to get back on her feet, while Jacob used every ounce of his strength against Tim. Penny knew Jacob's stitched-up arm would be hurting, and Arlene was probably still feeling the effects of Deana's earlier blow to the head.

But she didn't need to make a choice about which fight to try to break up.

"Stop! Everyone, stop!" Officer Wally McPhee strode into the living room, in a replay of his entrance just a day earlier. He clutched his service weapon in his hand but kept the barrel pointed toward the floor. The threat and the suddenness of his entry made everyone pause.

Jacob dropped his hands and stepped away from Tim, who bent over to catch his laboured breath. Arlene dropped the grip she had on Deana and left the woman prone on the floor. But Penny wasn't looking at Wally, who was keeping an eye on the fighting adults as he holstered his own weapon and scooped up the one Tim dropped. She, and everyone else in the room, looked past the officer, to the two people who had come into the house behind him.

Thirty-Four

"Gram," Arlene gasped as she stood up straight. "What are you doing here? And why are you with him?"

Mary Barkson made her way carefully into the living room of the house that was once her home. Penny watched the elderly woman take purposeful steps around Deana, who had partially sat up from the floor, but hadn't made any more moves under the close watch of an armed Wally McPhee. Mary lowered herself onto the cloth-covered couch with a sigh. The effort she put into every step was clear.

"David brought me," Mary said. "So I could come here and see what's happening for myself. And see the house one more time."

Coleridge Coleman stood in the first entrance to the living room, looking nervously around the group of people. Just a day earlier, he'd been fighting Jacob in that same room. The last they'd seen of him, he was being led away in handcuffs.

"Why isn't he in jail?" Jacob asked.

Wally shrugged. "We held him till she posted bail for him," he said, signalling to Mary, who lifted her chin up and down in a quick nod of acknowledgement.

"I'm afraid I wasn't entirely honest with you girls, earlier today," Mary said. Arlene lowered herself onto the couch next to her grandmother. Deana tried to get up from the floor, but Wally warned her to stay put. "I knew David was Albert's son for a long time. I always knew I'd wronged his mother, and that life had been a struggle for him."

"You were keeping track of him, weren't you?" Penny said, thinking of the newspaper clippings piecing together Coleridge's — David's — childhood. Mary nodded.

"My sister Lila lived in the Valley and she knew what had happened between Bertie and Annette. I asked her to keep track of the boy." Mary turned to Coleridge and continued her story. "Lila did for a number of years, but then, when your mother married your stepfather, she lost you."

Coleridge folded his arms across his chest. "That arsehole moved us to a tar-paper shack on the north mountain. What he did to my mother." He shook his head. "He always said he had saved us from the poorhouse, but we would have been better off alone."

"Alone," Jacob said. "She should have left you alone. That's what you said to me the last time we were here."

"You meant Deana, didn't you?" Penny asked.

Coleridge grunted an agreement. "I wasn't fit to be no father, and I got no interest in it now, either," he said. "Sorry to say but it's the truth."

Deana turned her head away from her father and the rest of the group. Penny couldn't muster any feeling of sadness for the woman.

"Having a bad parent isn't an excuse for murder," Penny said simply.

Deana snickered like a child. "I don't care, anyway. I'm only here for Aunt Kathy."

"It's Kathy that should have left me be all those years ago. I never should have listened to her."

"Who's Kathy?" Wally asked, looking among the people in the room.

"You folk here know her as Erin, but I always called her Kathy growing up."

"Erin?" Tim questioned.

Penny realized Deana hadn't told him the full truth, either. "Erin Riggings is Coleridge's sister," she said. Tim's eyebrows knitted as he put the pieces together.

"Wait, Erin Riggings is your aunt?" Tim turned to Deana, standing up straight again. "That means Ward is your uncle. You were auditing your own uncle?"

Deana rolled her eyes. "Why do you think I wanted to come down here? Aunt Kathy begged me to get the assignment."

"And that's why you were so ridiculously incompetent," he said. "You were purposely tanking the investigation into Ward Riggings' scam."

"Yeah, but look what happened when I complained about us," she said. "Our affair became an even bigger scandal, and the audit was all but forgotten. Now it's you who's being investigated."

"And Erin did the exact same scam at the Winter Carnival committee," Penny said. "Which you were also auditing."

Deana shrugged. "What can I say? I told my company I could look into both while I was stuck in this backwater. They didn't want to send someone else down, so they jumped at the chance."

Jacob turned to look at Coleridge, who was still wearing the checkered woodsman's jacket he had been wearing a day earlier. His grey beard jutted out hairs at all angles.

"How much of this did you know?"

Coleridge turned his pale blue eyes downward. "Never knew Deana existed until she came into my life after her momma died. I wasn't in no shape to raise a little girl so I gave her up to the system. She tracked my mother down before she died and then came looking for me."

"Annette was lovely," Deana said in a voice laced with sarcasm. "She didn't have much money, but she loved spending it on me. Her only granddaughter."

"My mother was too kind. It's how come we ended up on the mountain and how come you could take from her. I thought we could have some kind of peace between us. That's why I let you stay with me. But there ain't no peace with you, girl."

Wally McPhee moved toward Deana. "Stand up," he said. "You're under arrest. Let's go."

The police officer held Deana's arm as she hoisted herself off the living room floor. Arlene offered a hand to Mary, and the women stood up from the couch. She stopped for a moment and, arm-in-arm with her grandmother, Arlene tossed the unsigned ownership papers into the last of fire. Penny followed as the women slowly made their way out of the living room and into the darkened hallway.

"Mary, how did you know we'd be here?" Penny asked.

Mary Barkson paused as they crossed into the kitchen. She slid her hand along the doorjamb and looked back over her shoulder, beyond Penny and toward Coleridge, who was slowly following them out of the house. For a moment, Mary seemed lost in another time. She raised a hand to Coleridge's sunken cheek.

"I can see Bertie in your eyes, David," she said. Turning back to Penny, the moment passed. "After you girls came to see me and told me what happened with David and Jacob, I went to the police station to see about getting David out. I gave him permission to live here, too, while he fixes up his home. And I wanted him to protect the place if she came back to cause trouble."

Deana, who was being led out of the living room by Wally, stopped suddenly.

"You gave him permission? You don't have the right to do that. The house belongs to Albert's heirs. Vicki, Arlene, and my father," she said, her eyes growing wide. "He has a right to this house too."

"Is that what my granddaughter told you?" Mary said, her eyes crinkling with a wry smile. "Vicki always enjoyed stirring the pot. No, my dear, Vicki didn't have any say at all over this house. Neither did Arlene, although she did the work of maintaining it for me."

Arlene nodded in agreement with Mary.

"And I'm sorry to tell you, but as his widow, I'm the only heir to the estate of Albert Barkson. Vicki was trying to get me to sign over the house, but I refused. I told her she needed David's permission. That set her on the journey of finding him and, unfortunately, bringing you into her life."

Wally clipped a set of handcuffs on a cursing Deana and led her outside of the house.

"When I was at the station, Officer McPhee got your message, Jacob," Mary said. "So we followed him here."

Coleridge looked at Jacob. "I'm damn sorry about what I done to you," he said. "I would never have hurt your young fella. After my daughter tried to steal the old man's truck and set the house on fire, I was already watching things, and you folks spooked me."

Jacob nodded, although Penny knew he wouldn't easily forget the image of Coleridge clutching a terrified Chris.

As Arlene closed the door to the house, Wally placed her cousin in the back of the cruiser. The Atlantic ocean beat its steady roll against the rocks on the other side of the coastal road. Penny noticed a canopy of stars had come out in the sky, bringing a darkness that she never felt in the perpetual illumination of Toronto.

"Don't leave town," Wally warned Tim. "I want you at the station by 8 am tomorrow or it's a warrant for your arrest. I've got questions for you."

"You're not the only one," Arlene said. Tim stayed silent, clearly still astonished by how everything had played out. Deana had thoroughly played him, to capture a prize that wasn't even available to win.

Mary Barkson pulled her quilted winter coat tighter around her shoulders and looked to Coleridge, the man she knew as David.

"Will you take me back to Lazy Pines? And then you're welcome to stay in this house as long as you like. Until you and my granddaughter decide what to do with it."

Arlene and Coleridge glanced at each other and nodded. But Mary wasn't finished. "And Tim, this family is done with you."

He looked down to the ground and dug in his pocket for a car key before crossing the snowy driveway to the compact car stashed in the corner lot.

"Mary, are you sure we can't take you back to Lazy Pines?"

"It's fine, my dear. David and I have plenty to catch up on."

The older woman took Coleridge's arm and walked through the snow. He held her hand as she lifted her tired frame into the passenger side of his battered Ford pickup. They pulled out of the driveway, following the Shells Harbour police car into the night. Penny started her car to turn on the heat for a shivering Arlene.

Jacob was about to get in his own truck when Penny walked over.

"Thank you for helping me find Arlene tonight," she said as they stood under the darkened sky. "I never would have thought it would turn out this way."

Jacob shook his head. "I've known Tim for years. I can't believe he could do this to his own family, for a woman he barely knew."

"We have to confront Erin and Ward Riggings," Penny said. "I don't know if their fraud can ever be confirmed, but people in this town need to know what they're capable of, too."

Jacob looked at his watch.

"I know exactly where they are right now," he said. "After you drop off Arlene, come over to the fire hall. I'll be there."

Thirty-Five

As Penny drove, Arlene called Roger Truitt on the way home, explaining what they had discovered as best as she could. He had just picked up the boys from the arena where the fire department had won in the hockey game over the police. Zach and Jared had no understanding about why Tim had left them alone at the game.

"When I come over tomorrow to pick up Zach from his sleepover, I'll talk to the boys," Arlene told Roger. "At least we finally can give the kids some answers."

At home, Arlene switched on her water kettle and put a berry-scented bag of herbal tea in the biggest mug in her kitchen.

"I'd offer you some, but I know you have other plans."

Penny smiled but turned serious quickly. "Are you sure you don't need to go to the emergency room? Your head must be pretty sore."

"Peepee, you can stop worrying about me now. You've done enough for me and for my family. Thank you for all this, but you can go back to your life now."

Penny looked at her exhausted friend and tried to decipher her tone. There was, she thought, a tinge of hope underlying her words. Hope, maybe, that Penny would say the only words that came into her mind in response.

"This is my life now. Shells Harbour. Sheila, the bookstore, Jacob, Paul. And you, Leenie."

Arlene poured the stream of hot water into her mug and glanced at

Penny. "Are you sure about staying here? This town was too small for you once. How do you know it won't be again?"

Penny shrugged. "I think it was me that was small."

She left Arlene's house with a promise to return the next day for a drive back to the Barkson house so Arlene could pick up the car Deana had stolen. And Penny promised time for a coffee date at the Jungle Cafe to update on Erin and Ward Riggings. They were her focus now.

Cars and trucks packed the parking lot behind the fire hall. She saw Jacob's truck tucked into the special section reserved for firefighters as she walked through the cold night from the snowy spot she found in a back corner. Inside the fire station's auditorium, Jacob was in a group of laughing men she recognized as other firefighters, although her friend's face was stern and focused only on her as she entered. Jacob told her the police officers and firefighters always met at the hall after the game, a chance to have some Shells Harbour seafood chowder and soothe any tensions that might have arisen on the ice.

Paul Haines was in the kitchen, ladling soup as the players and members of the community dined on plastic tables set up around the hall's large meeting room. Tammy Johnson and other firefighters circulated among the tables, collecting empty bottles and dishes. Penny slipped in next to Paul and helped him fill soup bowls while quietly filling him in.

"My God," Paul said. "Is Arlene okay? And Mary?"

"They're both fine," Penny replied, eyeing the dripping ladle that Paul seemed to have forgotten. "Careful."

Erin and Ward Riggings sat at a corner table alongside the deputy mayor, Lowell Cranson, and another couple Penny recognized as owners of a bed-and-breakfast. She could see the interactions in the hall through the bar window that Paul used to serve the soup, although a three-piece rock band drowned out the din of voices. A few couples were swinging on the dance floor, while other groups spooned up soup and swung back beer.

Penny didn't see Sheila and Esi slip into the same side entrance she used, but she wasn't surprised when they appeared in front of her. Sheila had been her first call after she left Arlene's house. Paul motioned to another firefighter to take over serving the chowder and ushered them all to an open table at the edge of the hall.

"How's Arlene?" Sheila asked Penny first.

"She's resting. Physically, she's fine, but she's devastated and worried about how this is all going to affect Zach," Penny said. "He's very close with his dad and Arlene says he took their separation hard."

"If she's patient and open to getting them both some help, they'll get through it," Esi said, patting her gloved hand on Penny's arm. Esi looked at the rest of the group and leaned in. A few more couples joined the dancers on the floor as the band moved into "Brown Eyed Girl".

"I finally got a chance to speak with the deputy mayor," Esi said.

Penny glanced at the table in the opposite corner, where Cranson was pulling back another swig of beer. Erin Riggings, though, looked right back at Penny's table.

"What did he say?" Paul asked.

"He asked for my papers, and I walked him through what I had found," Esi said. "He pointed out that everything I was accusing Erin of could have been a misunderstanding, a mistake on the part of someone who's simply an unpaid volunteer for a small-town committee."

"This was clearly no mistake," Penny said. "Especially since her husband was running the same scheme at Prime Ocean."

"We know that, but Cranson will want to cover this up as much as possible," Sheila said.

Esi nodded. "He implied as much to me, asked me to let him handle it," she said. "I suspect after this carnival is over, Erin will quietly resign from the committee and that will be that."

"And considering the town can't trust the auditor they hired to look into all this in the first place, they'll probably try to let it all fade into history," Paul said, shaking his head. "That's politics, for you."

"Erin might not be off the committee for long. Ward's company, Sail Away, is a sponsor," Esi said. "He probably started that business with money he stole from Prime Ocean. But that's beyond our ability to find out and it seems like the fish plant too will probably want this all to go away. They've probably already written off whatever loss he caused as a bad debt, hidden from their investors."

Penny glanced over her shoulder again at the group in the far corner. Erin Riggings was still watching them. Penny knew Esi was right, that the Riggings would likely emerge from this with little sticking to them. And she also knew that she had kept her promise to Arlene, and the killer of Vicki Truitt was sitting in the Shells Harbour Police holding cell.

But she pushed her chair back and rose, feeling the aches of the last days in her limbs. From the corner of her eye, she saw Jacob enter the hall from an inner door that led to the apparatus bay, where the fire trucks waited to race to their next call. But Penny's destination was in a direction away from her old friend. Erin looked at her, sitting up straighter as she approached.

"Katherine, let me tell you how sorry I am about your niece," Penny said. Lowell Cranson looked up from the rim of his beer bottle and squinted at Penny through his wide frame glasses.

"You must not be from here, Miss. This lady's name is Erin. Erin Riggings," the deputy mayor said, his words holding a hint of a slur.

"I was born and raised here, Mr. Cranson. She and I have met. More than once," Penny said. "And I certainly know her name."

Erin Riggings folded her arms across her chest while her husband swivelled from his conversation with the bed-and-breakfast owners. His greying black moustache held a trace of crumbs from the bread rolls served with the chowder.

"What did you say about my niece?" Erin asked Penny.

"Oh, I'm surprised you hadn't heard yet," Penny said. "I thought you knew everything that went on in this town. She's been arrested for killing Vicki Truitt."

Jacob appeared at her side and surveyed the group. Erin and Ward Riggings gaped at Penny. Erin suddenly pushed her chair back from her table with enough strength that it toppled over, clattering with a force heard easily over the music. Heads turned as Erin Riggings swiftly left the fire hall, with her husband close on her heels. The deputy mayor watched their retreating backs and shrugged. He took another drink from his beer and turned to pick up a conversation with the shocked older couple on the other side of the table.

Penny and Jacob didn't bother going after the Riggings. Esi was right. There was little they could do about the pair and their financial scams. The town's gossip mill would churn away at them in time.

The band began the opening notes of "Rock Me Gently" and another group of couples moved onto the floor. In the kitchen, firefighters dished out bowls of chowder to the community. Penny looked at Jacob and moved out of the way for Paul and Sheila, who held hands and headed for a dance, leaving a grinning Esi alone at their table. Penny shot her a grateful smile as Jacob leaned in.

"Well, that's nice to see," he said. "They're old friends, aren't they?"

"They were more than that," Penny replied.

Jacob raised his eyebrows and smiled. "I have something I need to ask you," he said, straining to be heard over the music. "Let's go into the bay."

Jacob used his electronic pass to swipe open the interior door. The polished gleaming red and white units waited for the next time the alarm would sound, ushering the Shells Harbour Fire Department from homes and jobs, from the hockey rink or the grocery store, from the Jungle Cafe or the break room of Prime Ocean.

Penny followed Jacob into the small office, where a darkened computer screen sat on a wide blue desk next to a bank of radio receivers and microphones. He opened the top drawer in a filing cabinet tucked into a corner and pulled out a single piece of paper.

"Here," he said.

Penny looked at the sheet and then back at Jacob. "Application for membership? You want me to join?"

He nodded. "You'd be a great firefighter, Pen. You're tough and you don't give up," he said. "And you need to see that this town isn't as bad as you think it is. That we have a lot of good people who work hard for each other."

Penny skimmed the sheet, but her mind wasn't absorbing the words written on it. Jacob was right. Shells Harbour was her home once more, and even though she'd taken a bit of delight in embarrassing the Riggings, she knew there was more good than bad in the coastal community.

"Take a little time, give it some thought," Jacob said. "We'd love to have you."

But Penny smiled at her friend. She didn't need to give it any thought at all. She reached toward him and snatched the pen he had clipped on his blue uniform shirt and placed the application paper on the desk.

And she started writing.

Acknowledgements

With gratitude to the South Shore Scribes and my wonderful editor Debra Whittall. Deepest thanks to Sam Wentzell for his support and care. My mother, Madelyn, gave me the gift of stories and my father, Peter, gave me his love of firefighting. Adrienne and Theresa, my sisters, were early and ever-present supporters. Thank you all.

Emily (E.L.) Bowers, MFA, is a writer, editor, journalist, and volunteer firefighter. She was raised in southwestern Nova Scotia, has lived in five cities in Canada and spent a decade in Africa including eight years in Ghana and two in South Africa. When not writing or volunteering, she runs the rail trails around Nova Scotia, teaches firefighting skills and listens to live music in small-town bars.

To learn more about the fictional town of Shells Harbour, which is inspired by the villages and towns on the Atlantic coast, and get updates about Emily's work, visit emilybowers.ca.

www.ingramcontent.com/pod-product-compliance
Lightning Source LLC
Chambersburg PA
CBHW021329190726
48288CB00003B/1018